This is a work of fiction. Similarities to real people, places, or events are entirely coincidental.

MISS LOCKE'S CHRISTMAS SECRET

First edition. September 29, 2023.

Copyright © 2023 Anastasia Hayward.

Written by Anastasia Hayward.

Miss Locke's Christmas Secret

She has a secret...

Three years ago, a rake stumbled into Amelia's bedroom, forcing her to cover up the occurrence and hide it even from her family. Now at a Christmas party hosted by none other than said rake, Amelia is torn between staying the proper wallflower with a secret or blooming into the woman she was on that fateful night so long ago.

He is an open book...

Lord Orion Sudbury, a recently reformed rake, knows that the quiet woman in the drab dress hides a fierce personality. Partnered together in a contest at his Christmas party, he is determined to figure out more than just the mystery game's clues.

Not everyone is as they seem...

Together again, their personalities clash and the closer they get to winning the game, the more Amelia worries that a rake's curiosity will lead to her ruin.

Prologue

June 1815

The previous Christmas, when her mother announced they were going to London for the season, Amelia had been full of questions.

Would a season not require many dresses? Would a season be quite expensive? Would the air in London not be rather dirty? And smelly? And bad for her mother's complexion?

Her mother, framed in festive greenery, poised in her chair in front of the warm fire, had said, "It will be no trouble at all, dear. I have already sent off your measurements for dress orders. And of course London will be expensive!" Her mother clapped her hands like an excited schoolgirl. "I think the change in pace will be good for my health. It is not good to sit here, *wasting* away."

Amelia knew her mother meant that her appearance was wasted out here in the country where no one important ever saw her.

Her mother framed her face with her hands. "London deserves to be graced with my beauty."

The idea of a London season was as ridiculous then as it was now. Except now Amelia knew how exhausting it could be.

And how much her mother wanted her to marry someone.

Literally anyone. That young buck, this old widower, that man with the tipsy gait and horrid breath.

The more men she met, the less she wanted to get married at all. All the good men were either married already or not at all interested in her.

Mousy, little Amelia. She reads too much. Very nearly a bluestocking.

If she let her thoughts drift down this path she would never get to sleep and there was so much to do tomorrow. Thinking about it all was tiring enough.

That's it, Amelia. Think of all the exhausting things your mother will drag you to tomorrow and you will...

She blew out the candle.

...be able to close your eyes...

She snuggled her head into her downy pillow.

...and rest your mind...

She tried to stop worrying about everything all at once.

...and theoretically, you will fall asleep.

She heard the soft sound of her door opening. Then there was the tiny metallic sound of the latch falling back into place to close the door.

A husky, male voice floated across her bedroom, "Well, do I have a surprise for you."

Eyes wide, staring at the dark wall, wishing she was facing the door, she wondered what to do. Should she scream? Should she roll out of bed and run for the fire poker?

His voice sounded closer, now. "Are you asleep? I have ways to wake you up."

She knew this voice. He sounded so familiar. Who was it?

"Tsk, tsk, Mary. How could you invite me and then fall asleep?"

Mary? He was meeting her mother?

No, that didn't make any sense.

She rolled from the bed, sliding from under the covers, and darted to the fireplace to grab the poker. "Get out of my room!"

She yelled it. The walls of this house were horridly thin and sounds carried easily. Someone would rescue her at any moment.

He screamed. "Gah! You're not Mary!"

At the same time, she blinked and blurted out a startled realization. "Lord Sudbury?"

This man was a cad! He must have misunderstood her mother's natural inclination to flirt and mistook it for an invitation.

What a bounder! A completely dishonest, selfish, immoral...

She raised her poker higher. "Get out!"

He ran his hand down his cheek. "Good God. You're not even married, are you? They'll want to make me fix this."

He was right. This was bad.

An unmarried gentleman was in her room. If word of this got out, people would make all kinds of assumptions, none of them good.

Her father would expect them to get married.

She pointed at him with the poker. "You have to leave. Now."

But she had screamed. She had surely woken up someone who was, she hoped, already running to her rescue.

She swiveled the poker to point it at the window. "Out the window. Now!"

Rushing over, she set down the poker so she could use both hands to open the window. He was right behind her. She could feel his body heat through the fabric of her cotton night rail and it occurred to her how indecent this entire experience truly was.

He hovered just behind her shoulder and together, they leaned forward a little to look down.

He said, "I am not sure I can drop that far."

He stood extremely close. He had removed his neckcloth and her nose came up to his neck. His skin smelled warm and musky. He was a rake, through and through, and it was obvious why.

Her eyes were level with his full lips and she guessed, with all his experience, he was an expert kisser. It was one thing to judge a man for being an expert kisser when they were all in the judgmental realms of a ballroom. But here, in the dark of her room, with the moonlight casting a glow over his features, those lips took on a tantalizing new aspect.

His gaze shifted from the distant ground to her. "My, you are rather pretty. Like an angel in the moonlight."

He pecked her on the cheek, a warm brush of those expert lips, soft yet teasing. Then he swung his leg over the window sill.

He called to someone in a loud whisper. "Hey! You there!"

My God, who was he calling to? They couldn't involve someone else in this.

He whispered louder, "My good man, would you be so kind as to push over that wheelbarrow? I need to get down."

Now. He needed to get down now! They had only seconds.

The shadowy man, large on his own but even taller with his top hat, pushed their back gate open. For a startled moment, she was sure they were all about to be murdered in their rooms.

The man asked, "What is this?"

Lord Sudbury pointed, "The wheelbarrow, please. I need to get down."

The man pushed the wheelbarrow over and Lord Sudbury let his body dangle, holding onto the windowsill with his hands. The man said, "It's not far. I'm holding her steady if you are ready to drop."

For the briefest moment, Lord Sudbury glanced up at her and she swore he winked. He let go and dropped down, stumbling and falling onto the other man, knocking them both to the ground.

Her bedroom door burst open and her father cried out, "Amelia, dear? I heard a commotion! Are you all right?"

She glanced back to see her parents rushing into her room. Pointing out the window, she said, loudly, "These two drunk men stumbled into the garden."

Lord Sudbury took his cue and laughed. He slurred his speech as he said, "Hey, mate, am I lost?"

Would the stranger play along?

Her father stomped over and swore. "How did they get in? The gate should be locked!" He shouted out the window. "I'll show you what happens to riffraff!"

The newcomer removed his hat and, even though he was a story below, Amelia swore he grew bigger without his hat in the way. He yelled up at them, "No need for violence."

Her father sputtered, "Why, you, you, how dare you..."

He spun on his heels and raced from the room to go do whatever it is men do when they are so angry that words are beyond them.

Her mother remained. "My, dear, it sounded as if the voices were coming from your room."

Amelia shrugged, hoping the gesture hid the tingling excitement that reverberated throughout her body. A great deal had happened in the last few minutes and the sheer improbability of it all suddenly weighed on her. Her mother couldn't know that Sudbury had been here or the narrow escape would have been for naught.

Amelia said, "No doubt their voices floated up through my window." At her mother's raised brows, Amelia went on, "I opened it to yell and shoo them away, but they weren't listening." Her hands fluttered as she gestured out the window and she hoped her mother couldn't see how much she shook. "Too drunk, I think."

Even in the moonlight, she could see her mother's narrowed, disbelieving gaze.

Amelia turned away to look out the window again. "Oh, dear. Father is chasing them with a gardening tool. The very drunk one is laughing while he runs away."

Her mother moved next to her to look out. "He looks familiar. Was that Lord Sudbury?"

Amelia had so many questions. How did he get in? Was it through the unlocked gate? Why had he said her mother's name?

But now Amelia had secrets, too. She couldn't ask questions without risking exposure.

She said, "I couldn't say."

Chapter 1

December 1817

Sudbury was a changed man.

His drawing room was cheery in a way it had not been in a long time. The spacious room was cleaned and polished, a warm fire crackled in the hearth, and the gauzy curtains managed to let in enough of the bleak winter light that the room felt airy. Comfortable.

Like home.

Never mind that this was his home.

He said, "Thank you Charlotte, I really could not have done this without you."

The vivacious blond flicked her finger against his glass. "Sudbury, it is only the middle of the day and you are already this far into your glass." She raised her brows in a way that felt as judgmental as he was sure she intended the gesture to be. "Some things never change."

Was she reading his mind? Charlotte had an odd habit of guessing exactly what someone needed exactly when they needed it. Which was why he agreed to let her coordinate a house party at his manor in celebration of Christmas. He knew that if he left her in charge, everyone was bound to have a good time.

And he would have none of the work.

It sounded like a win-win proposition when he had made the suggestion. So far, everything was going according to plan.

He sipped his brandy.

Life was good.

If the Sudbury he had been five years ago had told himself that he would have a small holiday gathering at his manor and days of good, clean fun planned, the old Sudbury would have laughed until there were tears in his eyes. But the Sudbury he was today looked forward to the next two weeks.

Charlotte asked, "Do you want to hear what I have planned?"

"No. Not at all. I will be just as delighted as the rest of the guests when the activities commence."

"Do you at least want to know who I have invited?"

"No."

She blinked and looked across the drawing room at her husband, Henry.

Sudbury said, "Charlotte, you are here. Henry is here. So far I am very happy with the people in my house. I trust you." He waved his hand and watched a blush steal up her pretty cheeks. "Whoever else you have invited is fine by me."

She nodded. "But do you not want to know who is coming so you can greet your guests? This is your house, after all."

He waved his hand in the air. "I am sure I can greet people without a lot of preamble."

Again, she looked over at her husband. They locked eyes and passed some sort of silent communication that married couples understood. Or maybe she could actually read minds. He hadn't ruled that out, yet.

Charlotte took a seat in front of the fireplace, tucking her feet to the side and leaning onto one arm of the chair. "I have planned to hang the greenery and find a yule log. I also have something special up my sleeves. Do you know the author A. N. Neemus?"

He settled into a chair next to her, extending his legs to warm his feet by the fire. "Of course I do. He's that author who writes all those novels you women keep going on about."

She smiled. "Yes! I wanted to hire him to help me plan the entertainment, but he wasn't available. Not only that," she leaned over the chair a little further, inching closer to him, "his publisher refused to reveal any contact information."

Sudbury rubbed his jaw. "Isn't A. N. Neemus that author no one has ever met? No one knows who he is?"

"Yes!"

He laughed. "So the author may not even be a man."

Charlotte pouted her lips, clearly disagreeing with him. "The little biography says the author is a man from Norfolk."

"Oh, well, pardon me. If the biography of a mystery author who writes fictional stories *says* the author is this and that, then it must be true."

She pulled away and pouted. "You are making fun of me and I don't appreciate it after all the hard work I have done for you."

He sighed. "I am sorry for sounding so exasperating."

"You are exasperating."

She leaned closer to him, but her eyes followed her husband as he paced across the room.

Henry and Charlotte loved each other. Deeply. Ridiculously. They had met last year at another Christmas party and were married shortly after. Sudbury wanted to warn them that it was risky business marrying someone at all. But they did it anyway and, a year later, it seemed to be working well for them.

He said, "Charlotte." Once her eyes finally left the figure of her husband to concentrate on him, he said, "I hope you haven't gotten any ideas for this Christmas party."

She laughed. "I have lots of ideas so you will have to be more specific."

He swirled his brandy in his glass and slowly said, "I mean, ideas related to romance. I hope you have not invited too many young women with the belief that one will catch my eye."

Her face was a little too serious for comfort when she said, "Sudbury, any woman risks the chance of catching your eye."

"But I am not looking for," he pointed between her and Henry, "that. I am not looking to be attached to anyone right now."

"Why not?"

"Because I like the way I am and I do not want to change."

Her hand reached across the gap between their chairs to touch his arm and her eyes glistened with emotion. "I like you the way you are, too. I wouldn't want to change a thing."

He grinned at her and lifted his glass. "Not even the day drinking?"

From across the room, Henry called, "They're here!"

Charlotte stood with an excited cry and rushed from the room. Sudbury caught up to her just in time to see an efficient maid hand Charlotte her wrap. She dashed outside into the frigid winter air, clutching the wrap around herself and laughing.

Henry stopped by Sudbury and accepted his hat from a servant.

Sudbury asked, "Do you know who has arrived?"

Henry said, "You said you didn't want to know the guest list. That you could greet them without all the preamble."

A gentleman stepped out of the carriage. A young man, probably similar in age to Sudbury's younger cousin. The way he sprung out of the carriage, Sudbury could tell the young man had an energy that could keep up with having a good time. There was nothing fussy or overly dandified about him.

He nodded his approval and said to Henry, "I knew I could trust Charlotte."

Henry explained, "That is Mr. Laurence Locke. They live near us and Charlotte has become very good friends with his sister. "

"Did you say Locke?"

There were likely many families with the name Locke. It did not have to be that one family with the angel in the night rail. After all this time, he could still remember the dainty miss in her fetching white cotton, the moonlight on her skin, her hair mussed from her pillow, and her dashing fire poker. Something about her had stuck with him and he could very clearly picture those few moments.

She had been bold. She had been quick. And unexpected. All she had wanted was to be rid of him. At the time, when he would have done anything to avoid a marriage trap, he had readily clambered out of her window. But not before smelling the citrus scent of her hair. A clean, fresh scent. He still thought of her whenever he smelled lemons.

Amelia Locke. He had made sure to steer clear of her ever since that night.

But he was a changed man now. He wasn't the rake, the reprobate he had been. Surely that angel from his memory was married by now. And even if she was not, he didn't plan on dallying with random guests. That wasn't his style.

So it didn't matter whether Amelia Locke was married or not.

She stepped down from the carriage in a traveling pelisse of dull burgundy. Somehow it was just the right shade to strip the shine from her hair and bring out the red undertones of her skin, making her look blotchy.

It was definitely Amelia Locke. This woman had the same blond hair, the same small, pointed nose, and the same rounded face. But she was not the bossy temptress from his memories. Maybe she had changed, too.

Chapter 2

Charlotte brought Amelia to a small but pretty little room with a chintz reading chair and a matching counterpane on the bed. As Amelia changed for dinner, she couldn't help but be relieved to have her own quiet space that would allow her to unwind from the stress of a house party.

Sometimes she wondered how she had ended up so very different from her mother. Opposites, really. When her mother worried over a new wrinkle, Amelia worried over a folded page in a book. When her mother worried whether the new dress she had ordered was enough of a fashion statement, Amelia worried whether she would have a chance to discuss her opinions on the most recent novel. Finding bookish friends was hard.

Ever since that strange night three years ago, the night Lord Sudbury had appeared in her bedroom, her mother had distanced herself. She stopped caring whether Amelia found a husband or not. She stopped caring what Amelia wore, how she spent her days, or even where she was most of the time.

The freedom of it felt hard-earned.

Now, Amelia had a generous amount of pin money, abundant free time, and fulfilling personal goals. Her life was perfect.

She also had a very good friend in Charlotte. Charlotte might not be interested in books quite as much as Amelia, but she was a faithful friend and a fantastic listener. She didn't mind being the outlet for all of Amelia's opinions. Until she had met Charlotte, Amelia hadn't understood how precious a friend like Charlotte could be.

The best of friends.

So, even though Amelia had her reservations about the location of this house party, she agreed to come. For Charlotte.

Her white evening gloves were worn enough that they weren't the crisp color they used to be. But they were comfortable, so she pulled them on and smoothed the brown satin of her skirt.

It wasn't brown, necessarily. Well, it was brown, but the fabric caught the light and aspects of it looked nearly golden. At least, that's what her mother had said when she ordered the dress. For herself, obviously, not for Amelia. When the finished dress arrived, her mother had been so disappointed, claiming she couldn't wear a color as dull as brown.

Somehow, all the dresses her mother didn't want materialized in Amelia's closet. Amelia was too busy spending her allowance on books to care what dresses she ended up wearing.

Gloves, check. Dress, check. She patted her hair. Check.

She opened the door.

There he was. He leaned casually on the wall opposite her door, arms folded, immaculately dressed in a black coat, buff pantaloons, and shiny black boots. His attire practically scraped over the chiseled body underneath.

His short, blond hair was casually styled as if he had just run his fingers through it. Or had he literally just run his fingers through it? Rake that he was, he likely had another woman here and maybe she had run her fingers through it.

What did that feel like? For just a moment, Amelia imagined that she was the woman running her fingers through his hair, letting the soft strands collect between her fingers.

She tightened her hands into fists and folded her arms over her chest. Some men required her to be more steel than satin and she let that wariness leak into her voice. "Lord Sudbury?"

He smiled at her, a smooth tilt to his lips that captivated her with a seductive promise. He said, "I was waiting so I could escort you downstairs. I am trying to be a good host, especially for Charlotte's sake."

She had to look up at him and double-check that this was, indeed, Lord Sudbury. "How thoughtful of you."

He said, "It is nice to have guests in this miserable, old pile."

She glanced over the polished hallway, clean carpet, and beautiful wall hangings. "Your house is lovely."

The casual conversation caught her off guard. She had expected some sort of flirtation or joke. He offered his arm to her and she hesitated. He said, "The parlor is just down the stairs."

Slowly, feeling less and less steely by the moment, she accepted his arm.

He went on as if she were any respectable guest. "It is nice to have Henry around. Tomorrow morning we will get to do some sporting things. Gentlemanly things, you know. We're planning on fencing tomorrow morning before breakfast."

He would get up early to do that?

She said, "The idea of fencing has always fascinated me. The precision, quick thinking, and control over one's body, as well as measuring up an opponent to accurately quantify advantages and disadvantages."

He scratched his chin. "Well, if you put it in words it is all of those things. But it is all more of a feeling. When I fence, I don't think about each aspect that way, it all has to come together as intuition."

"Intuition. So there's this mystical, inner skill that makes a good fencer."

He stopped walking. Since her arm was tucked into his, she had to stop, too.

"Lord Sudbury?"

"Do you fence, Miss Locke?"

"No."

"Would you like to learn to fence, Miss Locke?"

Was he leaning closer to her? The moments felt more and more intimate as his head dipped in her direction, sending her heart fluttering. His focus was entirely on her.

She said, "Fencing is not something-"

He interrupted her. "I did not ask what society expects a woman to do or not do. I asked if *you* want to learn to fence."

She swallowed and met his gaze, searching for the motive behind his question. She couldn't decide what was there in his eyes so she simply answered, "Yes."

He grinned at her. That slow, devilish grin, except it was even more lethal because it was very close. "Miss Locke, you have made this party much more interesting."

Suddenly he began walking again, in a hurry to get to the parlor.

They walked through the open doors into the warm room. A few guests were already milling about, including some new faces.

One newcomer in particular caught Amelia's attention. Her dress of pale blue silk highlighted the blue of her eyes and her blond hair was perfectly curled and pinned to frame her face. She had lush lips, a small nose, and large eyes with long lashes. How could so much perfection be bestowed upon one woman?

This newcomer was going to make her mother livid.

Amelia couldn't wait for the two to meet.

Charlotte walked over from her spot by the fire and linked with Amelia's free arm. "Thank you, Lord Sudbury. I can take it from here."

He said, "Actually, we have something to discuss. A small change of plans."

Charlotte's brows rose. "A change of plans?"

Sudbury gestured them further into the room so they were no longer in the doorway and they stood in a small circle as if they would all share a quiet, secret discussion. Sudbury dipped his head forward into their circle and said, "Miss Locke would like to learn to fence."

Charlotte's brows didn't drop at all. "How to... Oh."

Sudbury went on. "I propose a competition."

Charlotte's expression finally relaxed until a smile spread across her entire face, her eyes lighting up with a dazzling light that Amelia had learned usually forebode something scandalous.

Charlotte said, "Yes, that is a splendid idea. We can pair each lady up with a gentleman to teach her. At the end of the party, we will have a competition!"

Amelia glanced back and forth between Charlotte and Sudbury's matching conspiratorial expressions.

Sudbury said, "I leave everything in your capable hands."

Two women entered the room, one older and one younger. The younger, in a plain lavender dress and with her black curls arranged into a bun, let her older companion select a chair.

Charlotte smiled over at the pair and then turned back to Amelia and Sudbury. "I will announce it tonight." She glanced around the room. "Right now, in fact."

She hurried over to the fire and clapped her hands. Amelia was still a little dizzy over everything that had transpired. Was Charlotte really about to announce something so scandalous?

Charlotte said, "I have a game for some of us. Any lady who would like to participate is welcome to do so." She paused and took a small breath, glancing around the room to make sure everyone was paying attention. "Any lady who chooses to participate will be paired with a gentleman who will teach her how to fence. At the end of our party, in two weeks, we will have a little competition, lady against lady, to determine who is the best fencer."

The beautiful woman in the blue dress crinkled her nose adorably. "We will learn to fence? Is that appropriate?"

Charlotte countered, "Would you like to participate?"

"I suppose I would."

"Then, yes. It is entirely appropriate for you to do so."

The woman shrugged and smiled, practically glowing. Amelia glanced around the room. Where was her mother? Probably lingering over her coif, checking each curl.

Charlotte quickly counted the raised hands and then addressed another guest. "Miss Belle? Please say you will join us."

The older woman next to Miss Belle nodded and then Miss Belle responded. "I will join."

Charlotte clapped again, giddy. "In that case, I will announce the pairings. For most of the activities, I will try to be fair, but for this, I am going to be partial since I want my Henry to teach me how to fence." She paused a moment to stare at her husband, who was smiling at her. "I believe, since they are the two who hatched this plan, that Lord Sudbury will be responsible for teaching Miss Locke. That means Miss Lawton," Charlotte gestured to the beautiful blond, "will be paired with," Charlotte scanned the crowd and pointed at Amelia's brother, "Mr. Locke. And Miss Belle, you will be paired with Mr. Sudbury, who should arrive tomorrow. But since you already know each other, I think his current absence will not be a hindrance."

Amelia looked up at Lord Sudbury, who was still standing too close for propriety. She had meant to spend the party with Charlotte and had promised herself that she would avoid the gentlemen, just as she always did. She was a wallflower at any and every gathering.

But it was hard to be a wallflower when Lord Sudbury stared at her so intently.

He said, "And just like that, Miss Locke, you are going to learn to fence."

She remembered wielding the fire poker on that night so long ago. Did he remember too? Did someone like Lord Sudbury, who probably had a whole catalog of interesting scrapes and encounters, remember that one measly night?

He offered his arm and said, "Join me for a stroll about the room, please, Miss Locke."

Chapter 3

Ever since she had brought up fencing, Sudbury couldn't get the memory of her wielding that fire poker out of his thoughts.

She probably had not meant to, but she had appeared in the moonlight that night as ethereal, the light in the wisps of her hair creating a halo effect. She had been both stunning and beyond reproach.

A man such as himself did not simply touch an angel.

Now, with her arm tucked into his, she felt so human. So much like a warm-blooded woman.

It had to be the images from those nights that had gone to his head. At no point in his life had he ever felt so drawn to a female.

She cleared her throat and he realized he had been strolling in silence.

That night, though, she hadn't wanted marriage. She had been paraded around the ballrooms by her mother in an attempt to secure her future, but she had instead, when the opportunity arose, thrown him out the window.

And here she was, still unmarried.

Interesting.

In her oddly colored, unflattering dresses, perhaps no one else saw her as she truly was. But he knew better. He had seen what she was hiding. He knew there was an untouchable temptress beneath the ugly brown fabric.

And nothing stirred his interest more than when he was denied something.

He said, "We will start tomorrow morning, I think. You can watch my practice rounds with Henry and then we will begin to work on your technique."

"My technique? Would I not have to start with the rudimentary steps? Surely there are basics to be learned before I develop any kind of personal style."

She was thinking too much. He already saw this as a problem. "In order to win, I want to learn what your strengths and weaknesses are."

She tugged at his arm, trying to free her hand. "And what do you think are my weaknesses?"

He let her go. They were in the corner of the room and he leaned against the wall. She had her back to the room, free to leave him at any moment.

She crossed her arms, waiting for an answer.

He shrugged and slid his hands into his pockets. "You think too much."

She gasped and turned a little as if to walk away, but then she straightened and turned her fury onto him. "Is that the problem? I think too much for a woman and you think it will get in your way? Maybe if I acted as if I didn't have a thought in my head I would be easier to manipulate?"

He was glad his hands were in his pockets. Clenching them into fists, he didn't want her to see how much her insult affected him. It stung, her accusation burning like alcohol on a fresh wound.

The thing was, he was used to this feeling. This was normal. He was constantly underestimated and used to assumptions being thrown in his face. It was why, so many years ago, he had stopped trying to fight being who people expected.

It had been easier to give in to being exactly the person the world saw.

A rake. A reprobate. At times, an imbecile.

He pulled his hands from his pockets and crossed them in front of him. "Are you normally so bold with your accusations?"

She startled and took in a quick breath. "I am not normally coerced into spending time with someone..."

Someone like him. She didn't have to finish her sentence. He said, "So you would prefer to back out? No one will force you to participate if you are not up to the challenge."

He could see her thoughts as they flitted over her face. First, her eyes widened. Then her lids lowered as she found her strength. Lastly, she grew defensive, huffing a breath and crossing her arms.

Now they both stood with their arms crossed.

She said, "If you men can do it, I am sure I will exceed whatever paltry expectations have been set for me."

He smirked. "Miss Locke, you underestimate how capable I believe you to be."

⁂

WHAT HAD SHE GOTTEN herself into?

Amelia and Charlotte watched Henry and Lord Sudbury compete, their fencing foils clashing and clanging as they moved down the long room. The windows faced east and the sunrise poured in, casting the room in a golden glow.

Sudbury's foil glinted before it dipped into a smooth semi-circle and caught Henry's attack. Even though they wore safety masks, the mesh material over their faces protecting them, it was easy to differentiate Henry's huge form from Sudbury's sleek physique.

It was also easy to see how equally matched they were. Henry had powerful movements and he handled the foil as if he whipped around a long piece of straw rather than a weighted metal stick. He reminded her of a medieval knight who could easily wield a hefty broadsword and carry the weight of his armor.

Henry was fast, but Lord Sudbury was faster. He had quick reflexes and his foil moved as a blur with very precise movements. None of what he did was a grand swoop or too dramatic. His movements were small, calculated, and quick.

For most of society, Lord Sudbury was known to be lazy and indulgent. Nothing about the man before her indicated either of those things. He moved with grace and intelligence, something that, now that she had seen it, she couldn't *un*see.

Is this why women fawned over him? Because there was something potently attractive about a man with a powerful body who knew how to use it. But it wasn't just that. It was the glimmer of intellect that had her riveted. He had finesse and moved with a plan. Every time he scored, she replayed his actions in her mind and followed the feints, attacks, and advances to see what he did correctly.

And she started to see his pattern. It was never the same set of attacks. Fencing was starting to look like a chess game, except with a more physical aspect. Chess in real life, so to speak. And Lord Sudbury was good at it.

A feeling of inadequacy sunk into her stomach. The men had spent their lives learning to fence. They were good at it. In contrast, she would look foolish.

Next to her, Charlotte clasped her hands as if to hold in her excited energy. "I am so glad we are doing this. It was a great idea."

Her stomach twisting, Amelia muttered, "I am not so sure."

Charlotte probably would be great at it. She was a good dancer, she was graceful, and she was a fast learner when she wanted to be. Charlotte would pick this up like a sponge.

Maybe it wasn't too late to back out.

Charlotte patted her on the shoulder and said, "I am worried that none of us stand a chance against you. You have been watching them and I can see you analyzing everything. You have a way of looking at these things and figuring them out. You're going to be a step ahead of us the entire time."

How did Charlotte do that? How did she say something so sincere at just the right moment?

Amelia said, "I think I am going to feel like a bumbling buffoon. I already know I cannot move and fence like either of the men."

Charlotte just shrugged. "Learning takes time. So does skill."

"You have certainly never been one to let fear stop you."

Charlotte cut a sharp look at her. "That is not true. You met me after I met Henry. He makes me so incredibly happy to be who I am. It is easier to take something on when you don't feel like you have to do it alone." She turned to watch the men. "I am here for you if you need a friend, but I think Sudbury is a good match for you."

Amelia choked a little on her own spit. "Match for me?"

"Oh, no! Not like that. I meant as a fencing instructor. He doesn't think things through at all and you overthink everything." Charlotte stumbled in her speech for a moment. "Er, which isn't a bad thing, necessarily. I like that you are so full of ideas. I just think, between you and Sudbury, you will strike a good balance. Which will make you a formidable opponent."

A formidable opponent? Amelia replayed those words in her head, liking the sound of them more and more. Maybe she could do this.

Charlotte asked, "Did you read the book?"

Was there a book on fencing they were supposed to read? "Book?"

"Yes. The one by A. N. Neemus. *The Mystery of the Heiress.*"

That book. "Yes. I have read it."

Charlotte smiled at her. "I assumed you had. I am checking that all the women have read it for the game I have planned."

"Everyone here has read the book?"

"You will finally be able to talk to someone about something you have read!"

Amelia tried to smile back. Of all the books she wanted to talk to people about, that book was not one of them. But that would be difficult to explain to Charlotte, who lumped all books into one category. For her, there wasn't much difference in reading a book on animal husbandry compared to a gothic novel. They were all just *books*.

She said, "I admit that I am a little surprised."

Charlotte rocked on her feet a little, a jittery movement she made when she was excited. "Just wait until later tonight when I introduce the game!"

Chapter 4

Charlotte pounced on her immediately as she entered the drawing room. "I have been waiting to introduce you to someone."

Amelia eyed a chair and sighed longingly at the secluded spot. She didn't have much choice but to follow Charlotte, who steered her in a new direction.

They approached the beautiful blond woman wrapped in a warm shawl of ivory colored Norwich wool.

Charlotte said, "Miss Emma Lawton, this is my friend I mentioned, Miss Amelia Locke. Amelia, this is the friend I met last year at my aunt's Christmas party. I told you about how we exchange letters."

She was so unfairly pretty that Amelia wanted to dislike her. Emma looked like one of the ladies in a fashion print. No one actually looked like those ladies.

Except for Emma Lawton, apparently.

Emma dipped into a small curtsy. "I have heard so much about you in Charlotte's letters that I am pleased to finally meet you in real life. I admit, you don't look anything as I pictured. I wish letters could include little paintings of what the writer was talking about."

Amelia snorted. "Like a children's book?"

Emma continued to smile. "Charlotte is always causing trouble. She wrote to me about when she had begun painting a room by herself and the architect walked in to find her up on a ladder with a paint bucket. I desperately wished I had a sketch of the man's face when he saw her up there."

Emma twisted her lips and widened her eyes, gasping in mock horror, her pretty face trying to recreate what she imagined the architect had looked like.

Charlotte laughed, too loud as was her style, twisting her lips and widening her eyes. "No, it was more like this. His mouth was so unbelievably wide."

Emma laughed back and it was hard not to find their amusement a little infectious.

Charlotte's shoulders were shaking from her laughter. "He was so red when he left the room. I have never seen workmen descend upon a room so fast with their paintbrushes!"

This must have been before Amelia became well acquainted with Charlotte because she hadn't heard about this incident. Now she, too, wished she had a sketch of the architect's face.

More people entered the drawing room. Charlotte said, "I should introduce you two to them. They live here so I was hoping Lord Sudbury would perform the introductions, but he is..."

Her voice trailed off and Amelia's mind filled in the blank with the multitude of words that could have ended the sentence: insufferable, rakish, selfish, indulgent, spoiled.

The women who had entered were very different from each other. She remembered them from last night.

The first woman must be similar in age to Amelia's mother. Her evening gown, trimmed in green velvet, complemented her brown hair and charming green eyes. Charlotte introduced her, "Please meet Lord Sudbury's aunt, Mrs. Harris. She used to live in the Caribbean with her husband."

The other, younger woman wore a long-sleeved ivory satin gown with lace hems. Her black curls were pinned into a chignon and she was probably the tallest woman in their group. She carried her slender frame with a quiet elegance. "This is Miss Nina Belle. She will be fencing with us in the competition."

Her height could make her a formidable opponent in a fencing match. Amelia would have to try to sneak a peek at one of her learning sessions to gauge Miss Belle's skill.

Emma's father entered the room and Mrs. Harris excused herself. The ladies all dipped into a curtsy and stood in silence for a moment.

Charlotte was the first to break the awkward silence. If she even realized the moment was awkward, she didn't show it. "I simply cannot wait until after dinner to explain the rules of the party's game to you! You have all read *The Mystery of the Heiress*?"

They nodded.

Charlotte rested her hand on Amelia's shoulder. "Amelia, here, loves books. The entire time I planned the game, I kept asking myself, 'What would Amelia think of this?'"

Yes, wonderful. Introduce me as that kind of person so they can all dislike me from the start. Nothing turned people off faster than the possibility of interacting with a bluestocking.

Emma's blue eyes stared and Amelia tensed, waiting for an offhand comment and turn of conversation. Emma said, "I think the heroine is a little ahead of her time and I found her inspiring. Really, both the women, the heiress and her cousin, were bold in a very appealing way."

Miss Belle nodded along and added, "Both women used their resources to their advantage in novel ways. I am not surprised that it has already accumulated a few scathing reviews. After all, how could those men at the papers imagine a woman doing those things? They call it unrealistic but I also thought it was inspiring."

The book had received atrocious reviews. The main character had been called selfish and the ending "overly fabricated." Those harsh reviews didn't seem to stop the book from selling.

Did these women really like it? A small quiver in her chest caught her breath and she had to take a deep breath to steady herself. She said, "I admit I have not been able to talk to anyone about the book."

Miss Belle said, "It reminds me a little of *The Mysteries of Udolpho*. There is suspense and travel and I want the heroine to succeed. But this new book is less tragic."

Emma said, "But they think she is a murderess. How is that not tragic?"

Miss Belle answered, "It was the way she handled it. She was confident in herself and her abilities. She wanted to save herself and she did. She didn't wait around for a servant or a relative or someone else to tell her what to do or protect her or save her. She relied on herself and in the end, she was right to do so."

Charlotte asked, "But in the end, did you not want, even a little, for there to be a romance between the Captain and Miss Logan?"

Miss Belle shuddered. "No."

Charlotte said, "But he was so determined in his pursuit. It was rather, well, manly. And attractive. He had a level of competence that I admired. I wanted Miss Logan to see those traits."

Emma said, "I am glad she didn't. In the end, Miss Logan was happy to remain unmarried. I think that is why the book has such poor reviews. What would the world be like if it didn't rely on women marrying men?"

Amelia said, "I think the world is relying less and less on that very thing. Some aristocrats marry for traditional reasons, but arranged marriages aren't what they used to be. Women are starting to have more power to choose their lives."

The quivering in her chest hadn't stopped throughout the entire conversation. This was phenomenal, discussing these things with not just one other shy bluestocking, but with a group of women in a drawing room. They weren't targeting her for her love of reading, they were starting a discussion based on something they had read.

The butler arrived to announce dinner and the group paired off to head to the table. The courses flew by, most of the attention on either Charlotte or Sudbury. They bounced back and forth entertaining the guests with conversation and anecdotes, each one poking fun at the other at very amusing moments.

An evening with either one of them wasn't dull but together they were practically their own show.

Sudbury sipped his wine and glanced over at Amelia. He was thinking about something. Turning away from his scrutiny and hiding her face behind her glass, she desperately wanted to know what was going on inside his head.

AMELIA'S GOWN TONIGHT was a purple twilled sarsnet, the fabric itself rather lovely. But not on Amelia. She looked more like a fresh plum, something no woman should look like, as sweet as they tasted.

Amelia likely tasted very sweet tonight.

She sipped her wine and turned away from Sudbury, avoiding his gaze. Had he been staring? He focused on Miss Lawton to check if she wanted a helping of the macaroni. She declined and it wasn't long before the ladies excused themselves from the table.

Charlotte had let everyone know that this was the night she would announce the rules of her much anticipated game. A couple of gentlemen weren't in a hurry to return to the ladies, but Sudbury was. He had nothing much more to say and he tapped his hands on the table in impatience. Henry noticed, good man that he was, and directed the men to the drawing room.

Charlotte's excited voice called their attention. "Now that I have everyone here, I am going to get right to it. First, I will pair everyone up. Then, I will go over the rules of the game." She had two stools in front of her, one had a gentleman's hat on it and the other a reticule. Charlotte eyed her audience until everyone was silent and attending. "I have all the names of the ladies in the reticule and all the gentlemen in the hat. I will pull a lady first, and then the gentleman who will be paired with her. This way, it will be random."

Sudbury accused, "If you wrote all the names, how do I know you don't have a special marking on them to make sure you end up with Henry?"

Charlotte pursed her lips and arched a brow at him.

He had a feeling she wanted to pair him with Emma and he didn't want that. Not that he didn't like Emma, she was entertaining enough. He had other ideas.

Charlotte scoffed at him. "I thought you would be more worried that I already know all the answers and you wanted to make sure I didn't play."

That hadn't occurred to him. But now that she brought it up...

She said, "Not to worry. I had the game written and organized by someone else and passed the game instructions on to the staff here for preparation. Besides knowing how to get us started, I am just as fair game as the rest of you." She smirked. "But if I am paired with Henry, none of the rest of you stand a chance."

She winked at her husband. Sudbury rolled his eyes.

He said, "Fine. I am sure we can all agree it is fair for someone else to reach in and choose names."

She held up the reticule. "You start, then."

He stalked over and reached in, swishing his hand around in the velvet lined bag.

All the papers were similar in size and folded over in what felt like the same pattern. He pulled out a tiny slip and unfolded it. "Miss Lawton."

Charlotte carried the hat over to Emma. "Choose your partner, dear."

She reached in and pulled out a slip. "Mr. Simmons."

Charlotte's eyes met her husband's. "This should be interesting. The first team is Miss Emma Lawton and Mr. Henry Simmons."

Henry came up and fished around in the reticule. "The next team will include," he paused to read the name, "Miss Belle."

Charlotte brought the hat over to Miss Belle. "Mr. Locke."

The next pair included Miss Belle and Amelia's brother.

Mr. Locke drew Charlotte. Charlotte eyed Sudbury while she reached into the hat. The odds of pulling Henry were obviously nil. "Mr. Lawton."

Charlotte and Emma's father were a team. They would make a terrible pair.

Neither he nor Amelia had been pulled, yet.

Mr. Lawton drew out a slip. "Mrs. Locke."

Amelia's mother drew her partner. "Mr. Charles Sudbury."

Amelia's mother would be paired with Sudbury's uncle.

There were only two women left in the reticule.

"Mrs. Harris."

There were two names in the hat, his and his cousin's.

Mrs. Harris pulled out a slip. "Sudbury."

His cousin asked it at the same time as he did. "Which one?"

The suspense was wrecking him.

She looked down at the slip and stammered, "Oh, er, I mean, Mr. Edward Sudbury. Well, isn't that lovely, Edward? We will have plenty of time to catch up on things if we are a team."

Sudbury exhaled an excited breath. There was only one name left in the reticule and one left in the tophat. Everyone knew who made the last team.

For the sake of the ceremony, Edward drew out the last slip. "Miss Locke."

She was poised. She even tried to smile nonchalantly, but he saw her hand shake a little as she dipped it into the hat. Her voice wobbling, she finally looked at him and announced their team. "Lord Sudbury."

Chapter 5

Sudbury prowled behind the settee, back and forth, moving with the grace of a black panther. Amelia had seen one, once, at a fair, stalking to and fro inside its cage, radiating the energy that only a true predator can exude.

She felt a bit like prey. For some reason, Sudbury had made her a person of interest. He thought to play with her like a cat played with a mouse. She had allowed the fencing competition to happen for many reasons, the first being that she genuinely was curious to learn.

But this?

She would have to lay down some ground rules. The sooner, the better. She had a feeling he would need a firm hand if they were going to interact appropriately.

And they were definitely going to interact appropriately.

Standing before the group, Charlotte broke a wax seal and unfolded a sheet of paper. She skimmed it for a moment before beginning her speech. "I know we are gathered to celebrate the Christmas season, but I also wanted to take the opportunity to squeeze as much entertainment out of these two weeks as I can. As some of you know, I have been working very hard at Blenworth House to make it habitable," she coughed and glanced over at her husband, "er, hospitable. Since I am not the type of person to attend to something without throwing every ounce of energy into it, we can all imagine how busy I have been."

Amelia wasn't sure when Charlotte even slept. Visits often included Charlotte regaling her with stories of working on something late into the night and Amelia usually went home exhausted having just listened to the things Charlotte accomplished.

Charlotte was the best of friends to Amelia, but that didn't come without a few pangs of jealousy once in a while. The woman had so much, not just energy, but feelings, friends, and fun. She made Amelia's quiet, little life feel empty.

But then Amelia dug into the next novel and everything didn't feel so hollow.

Charlotte went on, "I selfishly did not plan this game myself. It was a relief, I admit, to not have to worry about it." She laughed. So did Henry. "I worried anyway. But I think I made the right choice in sending my idea for a game off to someone else because I am just as excited, maybe more so, as everyone else to be able to solve this mystery. I have paired everyone into teams of two and it did not go beyond everyone's notice that you are all in male and female pairs. This is because the game is based on the novel *The Mystery of the Heiress*. Every female in attendance has read the novel."

Charlotte quieted a moment to glance over her audience.

Amelia looked over at Sudbury. He had not read the novel? He shook his head at her as if he understood her silent question.

In this competition, the men would have to rely on the information coming from the women. They would all have to communicate with each other to accurately solve the puzzles of the mystery.

Oh, Charlotte was devious, indeed. She now had the room's full attention. "The game has four puzzles to solve. The butler has the answer to all the puzzles. At the end, he will confirm the winner. Whoever is first to solve all four puzzles correctly wins the game.

"I do have restrictions, then, to make sure we are not sneaking around all night and finishing the game tomorrow. What fun would that be? Solving the puzzles can only take place after breakfast and before dinner. Also, if there is any entertainment planned during the day, then puzzle-solving will be halted. The clues must be solved as a pair so no one may go off alone and try to solve the puzzle without their partner. Teams must be together when working on their clues.

"And finally, you may not ask the servants or any other staff for help or answers and you may not share answers with other teams. Each team must solve the puzzles on their own."

In short, Amelia was trapped working with Sudbury.

Except Sudbury would not care about winning a game based on a silly novel.

Charlotte held up a finger. "Finally, and I know I said it once already, but this time I want to introduce the prize."

Prize? Why didn't she start with that?

"Just as in the novel, our game will end in a fabulous location. The winners will receive the services of a private yacht to take them to a villa in Greece."

Amelia swallowed. "Travel? The prize is a trip to Greece?"

She didn't think she had said that out loud, but Charlotte responded, "Is that not a fabulous prize? I didn't want to hand over a sum of money and since this is all arranged through Sudbury's solicitor, this is what we agreed on."

Amelia wasn't the only one intrigued at the prospect of an adventure to Greece. She caught Mrs. Harris and Miss Belle exchanging identical looks of yearning.

Emma turned her delicate frame to eye Sudbury. "I had no idea you had a private yacht."

He said, "I do not."

Charlotte explained, "The yacht belongs to a friend, Mr. Day. He has donated his yacht and villa for the prize."

Emma said, "But he is not here? I have never met this Mr. Day."

Henry, a man of few words, said, "He is often away from England. Thus he owns a private yacht."

Emma folded her hands in her lap. "Interesting. I hope to meet him someday."

Charlotte crinkled the paper she still held in her hands. "I will now, if I can have your attention again, read the first clue. It is a rhyme. I did not write this rhyme, so even though my rhyming skills are abysmal, this one cannot be blamed on me.

Kick up your heels
It is time to dance
Special tokens exchanged
Love at first glance

"And I have the first clue written out to be distributed to each team for reference."

She passed out a small sheet to each female teammate and then resumed her place at the head of the room. "Since it is after dinner and not a time to work on clues-"

Murmurs of protest interrupted her and she held up her hands for silence. "I know, I know. It feels unfair to me, too, now that I have to follow my own rules. But Mr. Sudbury has agreed to read aloud the first chapter of the novel for our entertainment. I thought that would remind us all of the story and allow the men a little bit of insight since most of them have not read the book."

The group waited while Sudbury's uncle took Charlotte's place.

Lord Sudbury pulled up a chair directly behind her and from the tingle at the nape of her neck, she would swear he was staring at her.

They were teammates, now.

Mr. Sudbury proved an animated storyteller, concocting voices for different characters and inflicting emotions into the words as they streamed from his lips.

Sudbury leaned forward in his chair, so close she could feel the heat of his presence behind her. In a voice that was barely a whisper, he said, "Tomorrow morning, immediately after breakfast, we may begin."

His breath moved a few stray strands of hair that were loose down her neck. She didn't dare turn around and find him too close for propriety.

Tomorrow morning, immediately after breakfast, she would establish ground rules. Breathing a little in relief as she sensed him backing away from her chair, she told herself she was not afraid to put a rake in his place.

Chapter 6

The light coming into the breakfast parlor was dreary and gray. It was a good thing no one was traveling because the wind whistled around the corner of the house and everyone shuddered at the idea of having to step outside.

Except Henry, who, scarfing down a bite of eggs, goaded the group, "You're not all scared of a bit of a chill, are you?"

Amelia sipped her hot tea and let everyone else disagree with Charlotte's sportsman husband.

Miss Belle leaned over and said, "What about you, Miss Locke? Would you ride out with Mr. Simmons?"

She blushed and sipped her tea, a little embarrassed to be caught wool-gathering. "You should call me Amelia."

Miss Belle smiled. "Then you should call me Nina."

Amelia nodded. "It's a very pretty name. I should be glad to call you Nina."

"You aren't about to tell me it's exotic, are you?"

"I, er, no?"

Nina brushed her fingers off, finished with her toast. "I am sorry. I suppose I get a little defensive. You have been so kind, I did not mean to sound rude."

She spoke into her teacup, a little unsure of herself. "I don't mind that you say what is on your mind."

Nina grinned and placed the tips of her fingers on Amelia's arm. "I don't want to get ahead of myself, but I feel that we will be very good friends."

Amelia set down her cup, her stomach clenching. "I feel the same way."

It was rather naive of Nina to put her trust in a friendship so fast, but it wasn't as if Amelia had loads of friendships in comparison. Most of the people she met ended up hurting her.

She left the breakfast room but Sudbury was nowhere to be seen. Of course, he would be late.

The hallway, however, was not empty. Her brother lounged against the hall.

He straightened and said, "Amelia. I wanted to check on you."

She waved him off. "I will be fine. Lord Sudbury isn't anything I can't handle."

Laurence crossed the hall and tugged on her elbow, drawing her aside. "I am not worried about Sudbury. I am worried about the game. Do you think you should even play?"

"What reason would I give for not playing?"

His lips tightened and his eyes furrowed into a frown. "It feels like you have an unfair advantage."

Why shouldn't she get to have fun with everyone else simply because she liked books? If anything this game was something she could finally excel at. She wasn't the most graceful dancer, she didn't have a musical inclination, and she was terrible at making small conversation. But this game? Something based on a book?

She said, "I would have to give Charlotte a good reason if I backed out now. She won't accept that I shouldn't play simply because I am familiar with this book."

Laurence began, "You should tell her-"

Sudbury strode into the hall. "There you are! I've been waiting for you."

Amelia hoped he could see her eyes roll even though he was down the hall. She said, "Lying to me certainly won't get me to like you any better."

He cocked his head at her as if she were a curiosity. "I wonder which is worse, your bark or your bite."

He offered her his arm. She accepted it, nodding her goodbye to Laurence as she turned away.

Now was as good a time as any to introduce her ground rules. She opened her mouth.

He leaned in to whisper, "I don't mind a bit of biting, by the way."

"Before we move forward, I need to convey my expectations of your behavior."

He reared back a little but lost none of his carefree demeanor. "Rules? I can play along. My first rule is that you drop the 'Lord' and simply call me Sudbury."

She nodded. "Acceptable."

He added, "And then in return I will call you Amy."

"No."

"It is only fair."

"It is exactly the kind of inappropriate thing that I want to set rules about."

He gestured at himself, laying his hand on his chest. "Are we not friends?"

What would give him that idea? "No."

He blinked away a moment of feeling, something in his eyes that betrayed him as an actual human being. "I, for one, consider you a friend and shall strive to change your mind."

"We do not know each other at all."

He tapped his fingers over hers. "I would wager that we know each other better than you think."

"Fine. Accepted."

"What?"

She smirked at him. "Your wager, I accept it. We do not know each other at all and therefore cannot be friends."

He stared at her mouth. "And what will I win?"

"You would win satisfaction in knowing that you are right."

Still tapping his warm fingers over hers, he said, "That can be what you win if you are right. I will demand a kiss."

She stopped walking and steadied her stance. Their arms were still linked but she would not take another step. "That is exactly the kind of thing I want to set rules about."

He grinned, turning to face her. "And you know me so well that you knew you had to plan these rules in advance."

She warned him with a low voice, "Lord Sudbury..."

His head dipped forward and his lips nearly brushed her temple. "That is a point for me and I am that much closer to my kiss."

"I will not take another step forward. Literally. I will turn around and go back to my room. I will read a book all day-"

"Probably wrapped in a blanket by the fire. I can picture it now. Do you curl your legs up to tuck in your toes?"

"I..."

She did.

He dipped his head a little lower and now they were nose to nose. "I think that is another point for me."

She was not going to let him think he could make up his own rules and use them against her. Maybe that kind of manipulation worked for him in other circumstances, but not with her. "I mean it, *Lord* Sudbury. You have not hidden that you have met many women in your life and you may think that you have been able to categorize us in ways that make sense to you. Maybe you assume that I like books so I am also x, y, and z."

"A bluestocking using math to explain things to me."

She ignored his quip. Hopefully, by the time she was done, he would be all out of his smart little statements. "Maybe you think that because you can make guesses about me and a certain number of them will be correct, that you know me. But by making assumptions about me, you do not see me as an individual.

"You do not know me. You have not spent enough time with me to learn the nuances of my personality. You do not know my specific likes and dislikes. And do not dare to presume to place upon me who you think I should be. You are not entering this relationship ready to accept the other individual in it.

"I have rules and expectations for your future conduct that will be followed or I need you to admit here and now that you are not capable of respecting me."

He had pulled back, staring at her, his eyes narrowing the more she spoke. "You think I do not respect you?"

"Nothing about the way you have treated me makes me feel respected."

"And you want to feel like a respectable lady."

"I am one. But besides that, I am not asking for more than what any other person would want when interacting with you."

His head turned away while he silently thought something over. Finally, he said, "I have been," he cleared his throat, "a very bad man, at many given points in my life."

She nodded.

Slowly, he added, "You want me to behave in a way that I am not sure I am capable of."

She was not going to budge. "That statement is a pile of refuse. Society has rules and I have expectations that I will lay out for you." She took a tiny step forward. "Sudbury."

His breath hitched and his eyes met hers. It was a little thrilling to catch him off guard.

She said, "I want to learn how to fence. I find your technique fascinating and believe you will be able to teach me quite a bit in the short time of this party. I am not opposed to spending time with you. What I expect is that you will respect me and not assume liberties that you have not earned."

"You want me to earn the right to kiss you."

She stepped back. "I see that you are not willing to cooperate. Thank you for making this clear and not wasting my time."

He cleared his throat and called after her. "I will rephrase. You want me to earn your friendship."

She halted, then turned and silently waited. He either had something further to say or he was grasping at straws.

"I know the rules you want me to follow. I have always known them."

She finished his sentence the way he should have said it, "You mean you have always chosen to ignore them."

He nodded. "I did say that I have been a rather bad man."

She crossed her arms. "You are putting it lightly."

He nodded.

She took a deep breath. "But you are willing to try to follow the rules and teach me to fence. You will behave as if I am just as worthy of respect."

He smiled and said softly, "You see, Amelia, I have always been of the opinion that you are worth far more than I."

Chapter 7

S he didn't trust him and she was correct to doubt him. He didn't trust himself most of the time.

Which is why she had been so very wrong when she accused him of being selfish. It wasn't that he thought he was better than everyone else.

She thought he had made assumptions about her, but by forcing her rules on him, she had also made assumptions about him. She had made the same assumptions that everyone else around him had been making for years.

He didn't trust anyone. It was easier to make assumptions, to never have to get to know anyone, to always expect them to fail you.

Henry was the first friend who had ever shined past that layer of distrust that coated his life.

The night he had met her had also been the night he met Henry. The man had, for some unselfish reason, pushed over a wheelbarrow so Sudbury could drop down from the window. He could have gone on his way. He could have literally left Sudbury hanging.

But he hadn't. And it was that moment of choice when Henry should have chosen to be selfish yet did not, that had cemented their friendship.

He had been in awe of that night. Not only had Henry saved him from a very awkward situation, he had taken Sudbury home, given him a glass of cheap brandy, and then joked about the women of London.

Neither man had been at a good place in their life. Or their night.

But together, their friendship had sliced him open in a way that allowed a bit of trust to seep in. Normally an open wound could become infected, disgusting, maybe someone would lose a life or a limb over it.

For Sudbury, the wound of their friendship had infected him with something nice. It was as if, to get better, he had needed a fresh wound that would allow him to heal correctly.

And that was almost how Henry's friendship had felt, at first. Sudbury had been so full of suspicion but Henry was too good of a man to let him down.

Henry was a true gentleman. An honorable sort of fellow that only existed in fairy tales.

It was strange to think that in this story, in a way, it had been Sudbury in distress.

And there was no way at all he could think of himself as a damsel.

But saved he had been.

And from that night on, his life had been a slow, unsteady climb from the pit of darkness it had been.

And it was all because this woman had practically shoved him out of her window.

She thought he didn't respect her or think highly of her. She was probably right that they weren't friends, but she had flitted in and out of his thoughts these past few years and it felt as if he knew her.

He didn't. She was right about that.

But she was here now and the insatiable urge to get to know her drove him forward. Who was this woman who had plagued his mind and turned him down that night? She was a person far stronger than he was. He readily admitted that.

The problem was, for as much as that night had saved him, it had the opposite effect on her. She had been so certain of herself that night. Now she was only a ghost of that woman. She hid in her awkward gowns, tucked herself away from people, and lived a quiet life with her books.

It wasn't right. Somewhere in there was a spark that was being tamped down and he was certain that he could fan it back to life.

Amelia was a woman far more amusing than she let on.

She pulled the paper clue out of her pocket and held it out so they could both read it. He stood next to her, careful not to brush against her even though it grated against his instincts to hold himself back.

Kick up your heels
It is time to dance
Special tokens exchanged
Love at first glance

He glanced around the large, ground floor room that, a generation or so ago, would have been used for dancing. When he was a boy, his mother held winter balls here, the walls decorated with greenery and mistletoe hung by his father in conspicuous places. "You think the first clue is in the ballroom?"

She tapped at the paper. "It says right here that, 'It is time to dance.'"

"And that fits in with the story?"

She said, "I suppose you will have to trust me."

He walked away from her, to the middle of the room and spun in a slow circle, eyeing every column, chair, and table.

He said, "This room is rather large. Do you have any ideas as to where the next clue would be stashed?"

"Well." She took a couple of halting steps in his direction, biting her nail and staring down at the paper. "It says that special tokens are exchanged. The heiress and the duke first met at a ball. Their first dance was a waltz and it was love at first sight."

He cleared his throat, pushing back dark memories that would quickly give rise to guilt. He had waltzed with countless women. He used to think it was amusing to flirt with them and then walk away.

There had been a monster within him that had no qualms about hurting others. If he wasn't careful, that darkness could seep back into his life.

Amelia held up her arms as if she would waltz with an imaginary partner. She circled her steps and glanced around the room.

He asked, "What are you doing?"

She didn't stop dancing. "If their first dance was such an important moment in the book, then maybe there is a clue to be found by dancing. We were all paired in male and female teams, after all. Perfect for dancing a waltz to figure out the first clue."

He followed her and pointed out, "But you are dancing alone."

She stopped when he took her hand and wrapped his arm around her waist, pulling her a bit closer than propriety would want but not close enough by his standards. He met her eyes, looking for any response that would indicate she didn't want this.

She returned his gaze and started to move her feet, prodding him into the steps of the dance. Amelia had purposefully not asked him to dance, but now that he was holding her, his proximity sent a fizzy feeling down her limbs, a little as if her body was filled with champagne. She didn't dance often, but with him, her steps were light and buoyant.

His arms around her were warm and his nearness quickly chased away the winter chill of the large ballroom.

The paper still clutched in her hand made a crinkling sound and she remembered why they were dancing. She forced her eyes to leave the spot on his shoulder and tried to look around the room. "I can't see anything now that you are in the way."

He laughed, his shoulder moving up and down a little. "I can't seem to see anything but you."

She knew that he could pull out all the right words at the right time to make a woman feel this way. He made her feel seen, as if he truly enjoyed looking at her, but she couldn't let his hollow words affect her. She knew better.

He asked, "Did this heiress and her prince charming exchange any tokens of affection at these balls?"

She glanced to the side, eyeing the chairs she would sit at if this were actually a ball. "In the book, he's not a prince. He's a duke."

Sudbury laughed again. "A duke? That is ridiculous. Why would women want to read about falling in love with one of those awful creatures?"

Her steps stiffened and the waltz now felt a little less fluid. He stopped dancing and looked down at her.

She said, "They never exchanged any physical tokens in the book."

She stared over at the doors that led outside to the garden.

He followed her gaze and asked, "Are you sure you do not need to check that they never exchanged anything? Maybe there is a small clue in the book. Is there a section you should reread?"

She shook her head. "I am sure of myself."

He stepped close to her and she could feel his breath on her cheek when he leaned down and said, "I find that the confidence you are wearing suits you very well."

His lips were so close to her cheek that she could smell the starch of his clothing. He laid a warm hand on the small of her back and said, "We've stopped dancing."

It was an invitation. No matter how she had ever felt with any other man, Sudbury's movements never felt like an invasion. His hand felt right, it felt comforting, and it felt as if they were now connected. If she turned and responded in kind, touched him back, then they were committing to some sort of physical reciprocity that would be difficult to stop.

She stepped away, toward the doors that led to the patio. "I think the clue is out here. They exchanged a token of their love out on the patio."

He held the door open for her, the chilly air biting at her cheeks. He asked, "So what was this amorous token?"

"A kiss."

Chapter 8

Why had she said it like that? *A kiss.*

She shivered and wrapped her arms around herself, the December air biting at her skin and the wind whipping loose strands of hair across her face. "Let us look quickly."

Sudbury, despite a slight reddening to his skin, appeared impervious to the weather. He pulled her over to a small shelter next to a column and stood in front of her, his back blocking most of the wind. "So. Should we practice the novel to gain insight into the clue?"

She nodded. "Good idea. We can run through the scene. They came outside for some fresh air and then she saw a flower she liked in a pot. They moved over to look at it and realized they were out of sight for a moment, the plant hiding them. Then they..."

He leaned forward, his arm braced over her shoulder on the column behind her. "Then they kissed. Alone. In their secluded spot."

She sniffled, the cold getting to her.

He stepped closer, his body warm, and his head dipped so that his lips hovered near hers. His other hand wrapped around her and pulled her closer until she was enveloped by a warm, admittedly handsome, rather seductive male. A smile slowly spread across his lips, a smile that twinkled in his eyes and it said in that moment, he was only interested in her.

That was why he was so dangerous. When he looked at her like this, he made her feel as if she were the only woman in the world and it was empowering to have his attention.

He made her feel special. Noticed. Appreciated.

But it was fake. He knew how to use his charms to make a woman feel this way. It wasn't just her.

He said, "I would love to know what you are thinking about right now. I have a feeling it has nothing to do with finding our next clue."

She snapped, "Of course that is what I'm thinking about."

"Why did they stop kissing?"

She stared at his lips when he spoke, mesmerized at how warm they looked, still a healthy, reddish hue despite the cold. They would probably feel just as warm on her skin as she imagined.

"Amelia?"

She sucked in a breath of painfully cold air into her lungs. "What do you mean?"

"Eventually they stopped kissing. I am assuming they didn't get naked and roll around together under the night sky."

Was he teasing her? She swore her body heat just rose at least three degrees. "Roll around?"

"They rolled around and then certain parts of him accidentally fell-"

"No. There was no rolling around in the novel. At all."

"What a shame. It sounds like a missed opportunity."

She needed to focus on finding the clue. Then she needed to flee from Sudbury before one of his overly flirtatious mannerisms broke through to her.

He asked, "Did someone else come outside and they had to stop? Did a bell toll and break the moment? Did he bite her lip and startle her? Why did they stop?"

She was staring at his mouth again. "Bite her?"

His eyes widened, the deep green catching her focus and she realized that he had been staring at her while she had been staring at his lips. He knew exactly what she had been looking at. "Have you ever been kissed? Not something a boy steals from a girl behind a bush. Have you ever received a body-warming, toe-curling, mind-numbing token of lust?"

All of his words cascaded down her body, settling warm and low inside of her, chasing away the winter chill.

He wasn't staring into her eyes anymore. His gaze very pointedly moved down to her mouth. "When you are ready to permit me, I will be more than happy to share such an experience with you."

They could do it right now. They were out here, alone, and he was so close. His words held the promise of a new experience and the novelty of it beckoned. It would feel splendid. How could it not? All he was waiting for was her permission.

She said, "That is not something that friends do."

"I think we have very different kinds of friends."

"They stopped kissing because the kiss was over." She gasped, realization springing in her mind. "And then he plucked one of the flowers and gave it to her."

He pulled back from her, taking some of his body heat with him, leaving the winter air to press in on her again. "So the token was not a kiss?"

She peered around his shoulder. "Is there a flower pot or something around?"

There, off to the side, was an empty pot. Sudbury reached in and withdrew a rolled slip of paper. She peered into the dark container, squinting. There were still quite a few slips in the pot, so their team was ahead of the game.

Sudbury threaded his fingers through hers. "As much as I am enjoying the smile of triumph on your face, we should go back inside."

She lingered. "We should count the slips, quick. We might be the first team to solve this clue."

He tugged and they ran inside together. She unrolled the paper and they silently read it over.

Their love has blossomed
Into something amazeing
Shooting arrows right and left
Here Cupid has been playing

Amelia snorted at the misspelled word in the clue. "It really is awful poetry."

IN THE SCENE IN THE novel, when the heiress and duke kiss, it had never occurred to her to question why they would stop kissing. The book does not get into any details since the story is conveyed not from the heiress's perspective, but that of her cousin. It is the outsider, the woman watching life pass her by, she is the one telling the story.

And that character wouldn't know why the heiress and the duke had stopped kissing.

But Amelia couldn't get Sudbury's question out of her thoughts. He had seemed so sure that kissing was not an experience easily ended.

But people kissed all the time without it leading to other things.

So who was right? The scene? Or Sudbury?

She assumed a kiss had a beginning, maybe a middle, and definitely an end. People who began kissing did not go on doing it forever. But Sudbury hinted that it evolved into other things. Things he knew about.

On the outside, she could convey to him that he needed to be respectable. But on the inside, the truth was, he felt like a flood that swept away all of her foundations, leaving her questioning herself and her decisions.

In the midst of the chaos he caused, new things flourished inside of her. Feelings she, admittedly, had always wanted to feel.

She hadn't ever been truly kissed. Not like he said. Toe-curling. Mind-numbing. The dangerous part was that she knew Sudbury would expect nothing from her. If she did kiss him, she didn't owe him anything else. They both knew that it would not lead to marriage.

There wasn't any commitment behind the act. Kissing Sudbury could be freeing.

And it wasn't until he made her feel caged that she realized she wanted to fly.

She didn't know what she was missing and the not-knowing ate at her.

It was the same feeling the announcement of the prize for the game had flamed within her. The idea of travel had always appealed to her. She was happy in her quiet life, but it had its limitations.

This prize offered something more. It was a guaranteed opportunity to experience something outside of her safe, little world. Her mother wouldn't be able to stop her and her father couldn't refuse if she already had the money and means. All she lacked was a traveling companion.

But if everything else was taken care of, then maybe she could hire someone herself.

She had spent her life soaking up descriptions of the world in books, imagining the Pyrenees, the clear waters of the Mediterranean, or the feel of the sun in another part of the world. But now she could possibly step outside of her books. She could step into the real world, an actual adventure, and experience some of these things for herself.

It would be like a dream come true. And once the prize had been dangled in front of her, she couldn't stop the flare of ambition that rose and planted a flag in her mind.

She wanted the prize. She wanted the adventure. Admitting this much had opened up her mind to wondering who this new, adventurous Amelia was. Where had she been all this time?

Chapter 9

The long practice hall was empty and the fencing foils beckoned to her. She picked one up, gripping it in her fist, the long end coming out between her thumb and pointer finger. The grip was awkward and she realized that she didn't even know how to hold a sword.

Not like this.

Maybe if Sudbury had been on time for her lesson, then she would know the proper technique for holding a weapon by now. But, unsurprisingly, he was late. If he showed at all. She should have known better than to trust him to keep to their schedule. She knew better than to trust him with anything, for that matter.

She slashed the air, smiling at the satisfying *swish* as the practice blade cut in front of her.

Behind her, Sudbury drawled, "That is not how it is done."

She whirled and pointed the tip at his chest, stopping him in his tracks. He folded his arms. "Go ahead. I will have you unarmed within seconds."

Would he? She knew nothing about swords, but surely just holding one meant something when going against someone unarmed. She said, "Would it not be unsporting of me to try?"

He laughed and uncrossed his arms. "Normally, yes. But I dare you to come after me. Do it."

She swished the foil through the air to whack him across the side. He dodged, spun, and clamped his hand around her wrist. She blinked.

He took the foil and looked down at her. "Holding a weapon and knowing how to use it are two very different things."

She licked her lips. "I see that now."

He nodded. "You don't really wish to hurt me."

She remained silent and met his gaze.

He sighed. "You don't wish to hurt yourself, at least."

She pressed, "You will show me how to use it, though?"

They were still standing so close. But he was late and she didn't appreciate how he wasted her time. "Is there a reason you are late?"

He walked to the wall and put the foil away in the rack. "I am hosting a party at my home and still have certain responsibilities as a landowner. Not everything I do is at my whim."

His answer deflated a bit of her resentment. "Oh. So what were you doing?"

"Trouncing your brother at a game of cards."

Her anger ratcheted back up. "You are lucky you took the sword from me." She eyed the rack of foils. "How am I to practice now?"

He tapped his leg. "You will first need to learn the footwork."

Footwork? "But I saw Charlotte in here earlier and she was like a swashbuckling pirate."

"Do you want to run around, pretending to be a pirate, or do you want to win the competition?"

"I…"

She wanted to learn. The right way. She didn't want someone to indulge her whims, she wanted to learn the real technique.

"I want to learn to fence."

He nodded. "That is the plan. First, footwork." He dropped his hips lower, bent his left foot with his toes forward, his back leg bent sideways, toes pointing out. "Mirror this stance and then I will come over and fix it."

She positioned her feet, right foot forward and straight, left leg back and pointed out.

He circled her. "Damn if I can tell what is going on beneath those skirts."

She blushed and looked down at her dress. "Beg your pardon?"

He studied her hair. "I am going to have to get you completely indecent. And I mean that in the strangest way I have ever meant it."

"I *beg* your pardon?"

"No begging necessary. I need the ribbon from your hair and we're going to do scandalous things to your dress."

Grinning, he stepped up and tugged the ribbon from her hair. A scathing comment was nearly out of her mouth but then his face changed. Gone was the troublesome mirth and in its place was a man blinking away demons.

He whispered, "Lemons." His eyes darted to hers and he said, "This would be easier if your hair didn't always smell of lemons."

She swallowed. Locks of her hair were tumbling down her neck and he had a heated look in his eyes that threatened to overpower her sanity. Just yesterday she had thought about kissing him. About experiencing what it was like to reach a point where a kiss didn't end.

He took a deep breath, the expanse of his chest rising and falling. In that breath, some of the heat cleared away. He dropped to a knee in front of her and picked up her skirt.

She stepped back. "What are you doing?"

He reached forward for her skirt again. "Don't you trust me?"

"I wish I did."

His head shot up. "You don't trust me?"

"Is there a reason I should?"

"I am down on the floor before you with nothing but the best of intentions."

She countered, "I do not know your intentions. I do know that you were late today."

He picked up the hem of her skirt. "So you don't trust me."

She shook her head.

He said, "I am going to bunch up this horridly ugly fabric and tie a bundle of it up above your knee. That way, we can both see whether your legs are properly balanced while we practice your footwork."

His palm skimmed her leg when he lifted the fabric and she sucked in air, realizing she hadn't been breathing. "And you are down there only to tie my skirts?"

He closed his eyes for a moment and looked as if he had just given himself a papercut. Finally, he opened his eyes again. "I am down here to tie your skirts so that we may teach you to *fence.*"

She handed him the other ribbon from her hair and he tied another bunch of fabric above her other knee.

He stood and immediately stepped back at least three paces, brushing his hands together as if there had been dirt on the floor. He stared at her skirt and she looked down at her stocking-clad legs.

She asked, "Well? Will this help? Now that you have probably ruined the fabric of my gown?"

He nodded. "The fabric was a disgrace to begin with and was hiding something very beautiful underneath."

He dropped into the footwork position again and waited for her to mirror him. Just as before, she pointed one toe forward and the other out.

He shook his head. "No, no, no. You have to bend your knees or your upper body is going to bounce up and down with every step. If your upper body bounces, your blade bounces and you are now giving up precision and control of your weapon. Your stance is about balance and the ability to move quickly, efficiently, and gracefully."

"Oh. Like dancing."

He nodded.

"I am awful at dancing."

"We danced yesterday and you were fine. Don't think of it as dancing with a partner. Think of it as dancing with a weapon." He laughed and circled her again. "I like that gleam in your eye."

"There wasn't a gleam."

"There definitely was and it was glorious. By the time we're done, you will bring any pirate you come across to his knees."

Her heart raced at the thought of that. At the idea of being strong and in control of herself and her fate. Not just quiet, mousy Amelia, but a capable woman.

He stopped circling her and then slid his hands over her hips, his large fingers splayed around her waist, pressing. Her body flushed with heat that pooled in her stomach. "Now what are you doing?"

He pushed at her hips. "If you would stop resisting me, I am trying to push your hips into a slightly better position to center your balance."

"Oh." She gave way to him, allowing him to push her hips down a little and back.

"You are a little too far forward over your front foot. You want to be," he pushed a little more, "right here."

She nodded because she didn't think her voice would work.

Suddenly he stepped back and circled her again from a few paces away. "Good. Now stand up straight and then get back into that exact same position on your own."

She groaned. "Are you serious?"

He didn't even smile. "You have no idea how serious I am right now. I need you to focus on fencing."

It was the only thing she was focused on. She met his eyes, stood, and then dropped her hips back down, bending into the stance. He crossed over to her and pushed her hips to the correct spot again.

He was right. She wasn't just thinking about fencing. She was thinking about what it would be like if he didn't take his hands away. What if he bent down and kissed her? What if she asked him to?

"Amelia, focus. Try it again."

She didn't trust him. He wasn't the kind of man a woman trusted. Yet here she was, trusting him to remain gentlemanly around her. And that was exactly what she had asked him to do. She couldn't take that back or the entire time they had to work together would devolve into chaos.

Fiery, passionate chaos.

She shoved down her thoughts. She hadn't come to this party asking for anything other than some time with friends and a few bites of pudding on Christmas. She had these grand ideas of winning a trip, of winning a competition, of being recognized as an accomplished, intelligent woman. But none of these things fit in with her quiet life. All of these things did exactly what she knew she shouldn't do, which was to draw attention to herself.

She positioned her feet into the proper stance, feeling for where her hips needed to be.

He said, "Good! Now that you can get into stance, we can practice how to step forward and backward. We will start with an advance. *Avant.*"

Chapter 10

For the first time in days, the wind had calmed and it was now bearable to walk out of doors. He breathed in the crisp air and was glad he had already taken a ride this morning. It would be easier to reign in his energy around Amelia if he had already exercised some of it away.

She expected him to be a gentleman and so far he hadn't done anything too terrible. His hands still practically tingled where he had placed them on her hips, guiding her into the correct stance. By some grace of God, she was a fast learner. There had to be a limit to the number of times Sudbury could put his hands on a woman and expect to walk away from the situation without being a complete scoundrel.

But he was a changed man now. Sort of.

She headed toward the garden maze and he followed.

He said, "I noticed you didn't participate in the musical last night."

She was covering ground quickly for someone shorter than he. "I don't sing or play."

Didn't all ladies attempt some sort of musical accomplishment? "Not even a little?"

"I do not like to focus the attention on me and if I were to sing or play an instrument for the sake of entertaining others, they would all stare at me."

He stared at her, focusing intensely on her face as if he could will her to look at him. "And you do not want to be stared at?"

She turned back and caught his eye. Blushing, she said, "Stop that."

They came to the entrance of the garden maze, the tall hedges green even in winter. It wasn't a large maze but there were enough turns to provide small nooks for any clandestine meetings.

Interestingly enough, he was not the Viscount of Sudbury who had designed the thing. Some other, previous, devious viscount or viscountess had installed this.

Amelia asked, "You do know the way around in here, correct?"

"Could walk it blindfolded."

Her brows rose and she was going to say something but stopped to peer into the maze.

He asked, "What? What were you going to say?"

"I..."

"You... were going to tell me what very interesting thought popped into that wonderful head of yours."

She stepped into the maze. "You do not have to stand so close to me all the time."

"That is not what you were going to say."

She fiddled with her mittens. "I had an idea. A joke."

He stepped up to her. "Your ideas are my favorite kind of ideas." For a moment, he remembered dangling from her window, all her idea. "What was it?"

She chewed her lower lip and looked away. "So, should we go right or left?"

"Amelia?"

"Fine. I was going to propose blindfolding you to get us to the center of the maze."

"Blindf-" He stopped himself, stepping back, surprise catching him with a pleasant thrill. He untied his neckcloth.

"I know. It was a stupid idea. You just made such a bold statement and I..."

His voice issued the challenge she hadn't finished. "You don't think I can do it."

The last thing he saw was her wide expression before he covered his eyes with his neckcloth, tying the fabric tight. "We go left."

He turned and walked into a prickly plant. Cursing and ignoring Amy's giggles, he angled a little over and tried again, brushing his fingers along the hedges to help guide his way. He didn't hear any other footsteps for a moment, then he heard quick shuffles as Amelia caught up to him.

She said, "I can't believe you're doing this."

This was the most unexpected thing he thought he would do this afternoon and the challenge of it felt like little prickles of determination just underneath his skin. Or maybe that feeling was the plant he had walked into.

He turned the corner, walked a few paces, turned right, walked into another wall, cursed again.

Amelia laughed.

"I am glad you are entertained by my failure at this."

She said, "I think this is the most wondrous thing I never expected to see today."

"Ow!" He backed up. "It was all your idea."

"You didn't have to listen to me."

"The thing is, Amelia," he turned right and bumped his shin against a bench, "I not only like your ideas, but I trust you."

He left unsaid the last little bit that he felt deep down. She didn't trust him.

For good reasons.

Which was a little unfair because he was a changed man.

She said, "I don't see how it would matter if you trust me."

"No?" He looked in the direction he had heard her voice. "I am blindfolded, walking around a hedge maze, rather at your mercy. I trust you enough that I willingly put myself at a disadvantage. You could suddenly leave and I might not figure it out right away. You could pull some sort of other prank. But no matter what you do, even if my disadvantage brings you immense amusement, I trust that you do not wish to harm me."

"Of course not."

He smiled at her, wondering what he looked like, foppishly grinning with a cloth tied around half his head. "This is the most fun I have had so far today, and it is now even better because I believe we are here."

He pulled off the cloth and nearly poked out his eye, he was that close to staring at a hedge wall.

She burst into laughter, holding her stomach and bending forward, pointing at him. "Your face! You got us completely lost but you looked so sure of yourself!"

He huffed with indignation, but her laughter was affecting him like rays of sunshine. He huffed again but with more mirth. "I suppose I cannot walk this while blindfolded."

Her giggles were trailing away and he wondered how to reel them back.

She asked, "You trust me?"

He nodded.

"Put the blindfold back on."

He had to calm the heat in his chest and the sudden tension in his belly. "Yes, ma'am."

She took his hand, her mitten sliding inside his fingers and her thumb gripping him, pulling him forward. He stumbled only his first, surprised step, then acquiesced to her guidance. He did trust her.

Women were his favorite pastime, but Amelia was doing her best to kick things up a notch, and she didn't even know it. He squeezed his fingers around hers, holding on.

She slowed and then stopped. He stood as still as a garden statue while she turned. She tugged her hand free and he let her go. There was a rustle of fabric, then her heat cascaded down the front of his body as she stepped up to him and lifted her hands to his blindfold, brushing her soft mittens over the skin of his forehead.

She whispered, "Are you ready?"

He whispered back, "Yes."

The truth was, he wasn't ready. Something about this moment felt perfect. He couldn't even see her, but he knew she was lovely.

She pulled down the cloth and her face was very close to his. He asked, "Are you trying to seduce me? If so, it is working."

She stepped back, tugging the cloth with her and it dangled like a white flag in the wind. Behind her, the garden fountain was empty, but in the center, a cherubic cupid pointed his bow with the threat of love.

Damn, but this woman was smart. "You figured out the clue, already."

She smiled, pleased with either herself or his compliment, he wasn't sure which. "I figured out the first bit when I was talking to Miss Belle last night. The second line says their love blossomed into something 'amazeing.' That word was spelled wrong, which at first was irritating because I assumed it was a mistake. But then Miss Belle mentioned the maze and I realized the spelling was a clue!"

She took out the wrinkled paper from her pocket and he looked over her shoulder while she read the second half of the clue. "*Shooting arrows right and left, here Cupid has been playing.*" She looked up at him. "I am sorry to say I don't know what this means."

Staring at the words longer than necessary wasn't going to help them. He circled the fountain to assess what in the area could be a hint. If someone were to create an answer and this was the start of it, where would they naturally go?

She was still squinting at the paper. "This must tie to the book somehow." She paced in front of the fountain and he watched her move back and forth in front of Cupid's arrow. "The characters fell in love, and this clue is mostly about Cupid, so the answer must have something to do with the characters in love."

She paced to the right of the arrow and said, "There was a scene when they admitted their love to each other." She paced to the left of the arrow. "They were out in a garden when that happened."

He asked, "Are you sure you only read the book once?"

Surprised, she paused and looked across the fountain at him, past Cupid's derriere. "Why do ask that?"

"You seem very knowledgeable about whatever aspect of the book you need to recall."

She paced back to the right of the arrow. "I hadn't realized." Then she paced back to the left. "They were in a secluded garden spot on a bench, surrounded by roses."

His shin throbbed. "There are benches in the maze."

She stopped to the right of the arrow. "Benches? As in plural, more than one?"

"Yes."

"I guess we can wander the maze and check all of them."

He rolled his hand in the air. "Read the last bit of the clue again."

" *Shooting arrows right and left, here Cupid has been playing*."

He looked beyond her to the path. The center of the maze was a circle and cupid's arrow pointed directly out one of the paths that led to an exit. He stalked forward and grabbed her hand, hauling her with him. "Follow me. I have an idea."

"Oh."

He pulled her along, turning first right.

She said, "At first, I am never sure about your ideas."

They walked down the path and he turned left at the first opportunity. There was a bench.

She added, "But the longer I think about them, the more I like them."

He eyed her. "It takes you time to trust my ideas."

"I suppose so."

He let her mitten-clad hand go and checked the sky, little bursts of sunshine breaking through the marbled clouds. He followed her to the bench and knelt to look under it. Built into the bottom of the bench was a little shelf that protected notes. His ancestors must have had some devious things in mind when they designed the maze. He never even knew the benches had hiding spots.

She put a hand on his shoulder and bent forward to look at the slip of paper. The familiarity of the touch felt like a brush of velvet against his sandpaper soul. The two textures should never mix or he might damage her. At the same time, she held all the softness he wished he possessed.

He cleared his throat, shoving his emotions down his gullet before he said something stupid. He held the paper out to her. "Do you want to open it?"

Chapter 11

Amelia couldn't believe they had already found the second clue. Talking last night with Nina, it sounded as if most of the party were still working on the first clue, much less the second. Her team was ahead by quite a distance and at this rate, that trip to Greece was assured.

She could already imagine the Mediterranean sun on her cheeks. She would forgo a hat, let her hair blow in the wind, maybe remove her slippers and walk along a beach. Despite having visited the coast before, her mother had never allowed her to do that.

But she wouldn't have to bring her mother. She wouldn't have to listen to silly rules or worry that somebody might think something unkind about her. She could go to Greece and be whoever she wished and not feel guilty about it. She wouldn't have to hide who she was.

She hadn't realized how stifling her life felt before now. She had never considered leaving home before. Oh, she had dreamt of it and imagined it. There was a big difference between daydreaming and fulfilling that dream on a private yacht.

No amount of imagination could turn the winter wind stinging her cheeks into a warm, ocean breeze.

Sudbury handed her the slip of paper containing the next clue. She moved to take it but he yanked it back suddenly. He said, "Wait. First, I want to know why you want to win. You are charging through this game with steely determination."

She held her hand out for the paper. "Notice the person who is now standing in my way."

He held back the paper, shifting it to his other hand, further away. "I am not standing in your way. I am merely curious."

She asked, "If we win the trip to Greece, do we both go?"

They stood like that, her hand reaching for the paper and his extended away from her, keeping it out of reach. She didn't even care to look at the paper, now intent on his expression. Thoughts churned behind his eyes as he studied her face and she knew if she kept quiet, he would eventually say something.

She wouldn't be the first to disturb the silence. But she would lunge for the paper if he didn't say something soon.

He said, "You want to go to Greece. To travel." He crinkled the paper in his hand. "Why?"

She pulled her hand away from him and settled her fists on her hips. "If there is an answer that you want to hear, why don't you tell me what it is?"

He stood up, his head tilted down at a rather infuriating angle. "I do not understand your motivations. I want to know why you want to leave. All I can do, Miss Locke, is piece together your quiet nature, your ugly dresses, your beautiful smile, and your intelligent mind and wonder what all these things put together add up to. Why would a dowdily dressed, quiet woman want an adventure in Greece? Which are you? Are you the quiet, bookish sort or are you a vivacious woman who wants to broaden her experiences?"

She pushed herself up on tiptoe, pushing her face closer to his. "Why can I not be all of those things? Why can I not enjoy reading sometimes and adventure at other times? Why do you think I have to be one way or the other?"

"Because I find it difficult to believe that, once in Greece, you will not simply hide yourself away again."

She clenched her fingers harder into fists, her anger tightening down her arms. She had to restrain herself from shoving him. "Hide? You think I do not run around socializing because I am hiding from everyone? No, sir. I am not hiding, it is merely that I like me. I do not want to pretend to be someone else simply to be around people who do not like who I am. I spend my time with the people who matter and I choose to find my happiness in my quiet life.

"What if getting to go to Greece is the freedom to be somewhere new, to be myself while I am there, no matter the expectations of others. No one in Greece will think I am *hiding*. Maybe I just want to see the ruins. Maybe I want to experience Mediterranean weather. Maybe I will visit a beach. Maybe I will read a book while I am there. I will do whatever I want and not have to give one whit what the judgmental Mrs. Preston down the road thinks of me."

She was sure he would have a retort for her. She flinched when he brought his hand up to her face. Softly, he brushed loose strands of hair from her cheek and tucked the lock behind her ear. The simple gesture settled the anger that made her feel like a taut string. She relaxed into his gloved hand and he rested his palm against her cheek.

He said, "I would like to know what you do with your days."

He was getting too close to her and he couldn't possibly understand the meaning behind what he was asking. A rake such as he.

He didn't care about her days. He would only wonder about her nights, which he had no business wondering about.

Except, he made her wonder about her nights. She had lain awake last night, unable to sleep, imagining the various ways he might kiss her and what it would feel like. There were many ways she couldn't trust him, but she could trust that he was a rake.

She had a proposition for him.

"WHAT IF, FOR ONE, OR two," she picked at her thumbnail, "or maybe three minutes, you weren't a gentleman?"

His heart thudded, he could feel it beating against his chest as if it were a madman trying to escape. "What are you asking?"

She paused, tilting her head first to one side, then the other.

When he had asked her why she wanted to go to Greece, he hadn't expected her answer to hit him so hard. She spoke of being who she wanted to be and not worrying about what other people thought of her. Yet for so many years, he had done what she had not. She was so much stronger than he was because he had caved and become the creature society expected him to be.

She had refused and was searching for her own happiness.

Could he, if he followed her example, do the same thing? She thought he was a rake, but he could be so much more than that. He could figure out who he truly was.

Find the man that change could make him.

Finally, she said, "Well, er, is that long enough? If it was just for two minutes? And then everything goes back to normal."

He slipped the clue into his pocket. She was so intent on her question that she didn't even notice. Hell, he was so intent on her questions that he was worried he would drop the slip of paper. "Long enough for what?"

"What if you kiss me?"

He was fairly certain his madman heart had left his chest because he suddenly had no breath in his body. Somehow, he sucked air into his throat so he could growl, "You think I can spend two minutes kissing you and then after, everything will return to normal?"

He was good at kissing. Maybe it was his pride, but if he kissed her, he wanted it to brand them with all of the pent-up passion he had been holding back. There would be no way he could kiss her for any amount of time and then pretend it didn't happen.

But she thought he could. Because he was a rake. That was what he did.

He should be able to do exactly what she was asking. The struggle between what she wanted from him and what he wanted to feel warred inside of him. Maybe it was his madman heart that kept him in balance. That devilish organ should return anytime now.

Between his traitorous heart and his brain, one of them needed to make a decision.

He could be a rake if that was what she wanted. He placed his hand behind her back, pulling her to him. The length of her body pressed against him, sending warm currents of lust through him. He willed that lust into his breath, into his voice.

"Do you think, after I ravish you for two minutes, that absolutely anything will be what it was? If I were to kiss you, Amelia, you wouldn't be the same woman you are right now. There would be no going back."

He meant it as a warning. He meant to scare her away. He meant to show her, for just a moment, what it was like for him to be the man he hid from her.

Her eyes lit, bright with interest. Her pupils dilated and, whether she knew it or not, she was a woman ready for two minutes of passion.

And damn him, he now saw his error. He had meant to scare her away. Instead, he had awakened the minx she hid behind her quiet facade. She saw him for what he was and she still wanted him anyway.

He rasped, "You ask too much of me."

She heard the rejection in the comment. Pulling away, her face twisted.

He wanted to yank her back to him.

She waved her hand down her exquisite body. "I know I'm just a wallflower but I want more." She deflated, the minx from a moment ago fading fast and a withered look overtaking her form. "I suppose there is a good reason why I have never been kissed."

He had hurt her. He hadn't jumped at the idea of kissing her, and for trying to be a gentleman, for not hauling her body on the wild ride he wanted, she was upset. He was damned if he did or damned if he didn't.

So what was stopping him? Why didn't he do exactly what he wanted? What she wanted?

Because he was a changed man. And he wanted a lot more than two minutes with her.

He took a deep breath. "I want…"

He knew exactly what he wanted but he couldn't say it out loud. He never, ever dreamed that Amelia would make such a bold move. That she could be a vivacious, curious woman who was willing to ask for exactly what she wanted.

And he had ruined her moment because he wanted even more than she knew.

She wiped a tear from her cheek and sniffled, turning from him and walking away.

Chapter 12

Amelia wished she didn't have to be so delicate with where she stabbed her sewing needle. It grated that Charlotte was her usual chipper self. Why did everyone have to be so joyful at a Christmas party?

They were making charitable items to be sent to the parish, mostly for local children, based on the size of the tiny shirt Amelia sewed.

It was entirely his fault she was miserable. It felt like a grayish, pulsing pit sat in her stomach, leeching away her energy and ambition.

She had wanted to win the trip but this wasn't a fun party game anymore. The stakes were too high. If the prize had been, say, a pretty item from Wedgwood or a Norwich shawl, those would have been all in good fun.

But an entire trip to Greece? Leaving her life behind? Experiencing the world? She had many reasons that enticed her to play beyond the realm of a parlor game.

She stabbed her needle through the inner seam, hemming the neck of the shirt. Whichever child received this shoddily hemmed shirt must really need it. It was hard to concentrate on neat stitches, on keeping the fabric folded, on not stabbing herself when she desperately wanted to sit alone in her room and let her emotions overflow.

Charlotte moved seats, a small pantalette leg trailing down from her bundle of sewing materials, and deposited herself next to Amelia. She leaned in to quietly ask, "Is everything all right?"

Another needle jab. "Everything is splendid."

"You can tell me about it, you know. Everyone might hear part of it soon, anyway, since you keep muttering to yourself."

Amelia paused. "I what?"

Charlotte arranged the tiny pair of pantalettes in her lap to resume sewing. "If it has to do with Sudbury, you just have to say the word."

She repeated his name, the bitterness of it rolling off her tongue. "Sudbury."

"I knew it! That man cannot last two minutes without causing trouble, much less two weeks at his own party."

Amelia smiled and placed another stitch. "It is more your party."

"And I am doing a fine job of it."

Besides the outlandish prize for the game, the party was entertaining. "Emma has the voice of an angel. The musical the other night was lovely."

"You should tell her that. She hates performing for other people and hates being the center of attention."

The beautiful, perfect Miss Emma Lawton didn't want to be the center of attention? What reason could she possibly have for hiding?

Charlotte added, "Your mother also played beautifully on the harp."

"Oh, do not tell Mama. It all just goes to her head."

Charlotte laughed, added a few stitches, then said, "I know you are partnered with him for the fencing lessons and the game. But it appeared as if you two could handle each other. I knew you would not let Sudbury get away with his usual antics, so I thought you would be a safe partner. Was I wrong?"

Yes. "I hoped I could drop out of the fencing competition and continue with the game on my own."

"Hmmm." Charlotte finished sewing down the pantalette leg. "I am worried that would not be fair to the rest of the couples playing. Of course some of us would be better off working on our own. Remember I am paired with Emma's father and he has no inspiration."

Charlotte was right. Not all of the teams were fair but they were all still required to follow the rules. Amelia said, "Mama probably didn't read the book. But she would still tell everyone she had."

Charlotte nodded and tied off her thread. "Do you know why I like you so much?"

The question startled her and she poked her finger trying to thread the needle through. "What?"

"Last year, I played snapdragon with Henry for the first time. I was scared to play because the fire looked dangerous. You remind me a little of the game. We are friends and it is fun knowing you. But there is something about you, like playing with fire, that I find intriguing.

"I expected that you would eventually hit a rough patch with Sudbury because he is who he is. I did not expect that you would give up. Backing out of the competition and doing the game by yourself is the easy route."

This was not what she needed to hear from her friend. She didn't need confusing drivel about fires and giving up and taking the easy route.

She didn't even think she wanted the plum pudding anymore. She wanted to go home.

At least when she was at home, she knew who she was. Before coming here, she hadn't been unhappy with where she lived, who she spent her time with, or what she wore. She had been not only content but satisfied with her life and her accomplishments.

It was Sudbury who confused her.

And she had let him.

She had given him boundaries and he had pushed the limits of those boundaries, which she had fully expected. What she hadn't expected was her reaction to those little tests. She had wondered at them. He had pushed and she had given way.

She had gone so far over the wall that she had run right into a field of trouble. Asking him to kiss her? That had been her idiotic idea.

Amelia wasn't sure about Charlotte's nonsense about playing with fire, but her friend was right in assuming that Amelia could handle Sudbury. She had to stick to her rules.

She asked, "Do you still play snapdragon?"

Charlotte had started to hem around the bottom of the pantalette. "We've been playing late at night in the kitchen."

"And is it, er, I mean..."

"Do you want to join us? I shall fetch you. I didn't know you played."

"It is impossible to be a complete and utter lady when one has a brother."

Charlotte smirked down at her work. She had quite a few sisters. "I think any sibling is capable of bringing out who we truly are."

⚜

HE WAS ABOUT TO DUCK into his study, away from the swishing sound of slippers across marble. Whoever was after him needed to wait.

"Sudbury! I have been looking for you."

He knocked his knuckles against the wooden trim around his door. So close. "Charlotte! Come in."

Settling in behind his desk, his feet propped up on the corner of it, he idly shuffled his letters around.

Charlotte never lost her rigid posture as she sat so he knew that she knew everything. Or at least, that she knew part of it. She said, "I think you know why I am here."

He nodded once, wishing he had grabbed a glass of brandy.

"I think you know what I would like you to do about it." She held her finger up to stall his response. Not that he had one. "Let me clarify that what you think I want you to do and what I actually want you to do are two very different things."

Her words swam in his head like a boy stirring a murky puddle.

She said, "I like Miss Locke."

He nodded.

"A lot. I consider her a dear friend and even if we did not live near each other I would write to her. And visit. Because she is important to me. Do you understand what I am trying to convey?"

Amelia was important. He nodded along. No argument from him so far.

"Right now, she is not happy. Do you know where I place that blame? I am not here because I think *I* have done anything wrong."

Finally, he managed to get a word in. "Of course not."

Charlotte pursed her lips. Was she unsatisfied with his answer? How much longer would she stay? He shuffled his letters around again.

Charlotte sighed and slumped back into her chair. At least she was done playing the irritated mama. She said, "I want to remind you that there is no cheating. I have noticed you speaking with the butler a bit more than expected."

"I like my butler."

Her voice deepened with warning. "Sudbury."

He said, "I have been rather good around Miss Locke. I think she is a perfectly respectable young lady and I plan to continue treating her as such. I have locked away all my bad behavior in a tiny wooden box, I then swallowed the key, and I promise not to retrieve it until after your lovely party is all done."

Charlotte eyed him.

"I also realize that I am not perfect. I plan to make that up to Miss Locke."

"You do." She didn't ask it. Her voice carried skepticism and doubt that pricked at his pride.

"Yes. I do. Now if you don't mind, I do still have an estate to run, party or not."

Charlotte asked, "Do you not have an estate manager?"

Sudbury smiled at her and shooed her away by wiggling his fingers at her. "I gave him leave to visit his family for the holiday."

Chapter 13

Sudbury had the dratted clue and she couldn't continue without him since she didn't know what the clue said. Luckily for her, not everyone had found the second clue yet, so their slips would still be hiding under the bench.

She crouched down to retrieve a slip.

"Amelia?" A familiar female voice behind her made her pause. "Whatever are you doing on the ground?"

Slowly she stood and brushed at her skirt, Sudbury's phrase echoing in her head. *The fabric was a disgrace to begin with.*

She tried to smile, feeling a little like she was sewing on a bow to cover a rip in a dress. Eventually, someone would notice.

Nina wore a fur-lined pelisse and warm walking boots. She smiled, but her face was shaded under her hat, her dark curls tucked back to cover her ears. "You know we are only to look for clues if we are with our partner."

"Oh. I, er, well..."

Nina laughed. "Do not worry. Your brother and I have been making good progress so I will keep your secret just this once."

She flushed, uncertain of what to say. Nina had been very friendly so far and Amelia wanted to say she even liked her. They had discussed a few novels last night and stuck together on a little tour of the house.

She didn't want to scare her friend away, but she did want to retrieve her clue. She decided to latch onto the familiar topic. "I hope Laurence has been treating you well. I know none of us could pick our partners and you and he had never before met. My brother can be obtuse at times."

Nina cleared her throat. "He is, has been, a perfect gentleman. No need to worry about him."

"A perfect gentleman? That doesn't sound like my brother at all."

Nina shifted away a little. "He has been perfectly respectable."

That comment hit a little too close to home. She knew of another man who was irritating in how he chose to act respectfully only in the moments suitable for him. "Nina?" She didn't respond and Amelia chose her next words carefully. "Has everyone at the party been respectful?"

"Oh, yes. This party has been as much fun as Charlotte promised."

"That is good. I..."

Now it was awkward. She probably shouldn't have said anything. If she didn't care about Nina, it would be easy to ask for space and grab a slip of paper.

But something didn't look quite right with Nina. Why was she walking alone out in the maze on a frigid day like today?

Nina sniffled. "It was nice of you to ask about me. You do not have to look like you just swallowed the wrong way."

Words continued to rush out of her mouth and she still wasn't sure she should be saying them. "It is just that if Laurence is being the perfect gentleman, then that makes me concerned. I know that sounds strange. I would want him to treat you..."

She wanted to melt into the gravel and slither away.

Nina said, "I know. I cannot help how people react to the way I look."

Amelia fiddled with her skirt. "Which is very pretty, by the way. Your bonnet is gorgeous."

Nina gave a disbelieving snort and stepped forward. "Will you accompany me back inside? The bonnet may be pretty but it is no longer as warm as I had hoped."

"Of course."

They walked side by side out of the maze. Nina asked, "Would you like to hear what I remember about the Caribbean?"

Another place Amelia had never been and could only dream about. "That would be lovely."

SHE NEEDED PAPER.

The butler pointed out a door that he said was Sudbury's study. She could take whatever she needed and bring it back to her room if she wished.

She pushed open the door.

A drawling, ribald male singing voice assaulted her, "...and a lovely bunch of..." The voice trailed off and Sudbury blinked at her from his spot on the floor, his back against the far wall. "Whutter you doing?"

She refused to step into the room and would have to find paper somewhere else. "I assumed the room was empty. I apologize."

He pointed and slurred, "Close the door!"

She swung around, grabbing the handle to slam it shut behind her.

"No, wait! Donchya want yer clue?"

Of all the things he could have said, he had to say the one thing that would give her pause. She checked the hall, up and down, then quietly stepped into the room and closed the door behind her for secrecy. "Well? Do you have it?"

"Yesh I do!" He grinned at her, but the expression slowly soured and he set down his empty glass with a thud. Suddenly sounding a little more sober, he said, "Don't look at me like that."

"What, can you turn the sobriety on and off at a whim?"

He dug around in the pocket of his breeches and then held the rolled slip of paper out. "I was going to ask you to work with me, still. But I can't. I can't do this one."

She took the clue and read,

> *"This now remains unoccupied*
> *The tragedy found here*
> *In this room without a view*
> *Tread carefully for fear."*

A room without a view? That sounded familiar. Perhaps from the small house tour everyone had been given yesterday? The butler made sure to show a few key parts of the house and even pointed out the maze out a window, stopping so everyone could see out.

Had he shown a room without a window?

Sudbury said, "I can tell your mind is already working on the clue. Go ahead, Miss Locke. Race onward."

She looked down at him, his arms limp at his sides, his hands resting on the floor. His head lolled to the side while he stared at a spot on the carpet.

She wanted to do this without him. It was what she had wanted from the beginning. But, for as annoying as he could be, he had his uses. After all, he had figured out which bench held the last clue.

They didn't work well together, but they didn't *not* work.

She settled onto the floor next to him, pulling her skirts about her so she could sit, then she took his hand and stroked over his knuckles.

Sudbury closed his eyes. "Frith will lose his job over this one. He has overstepped in his role as a butler."

She stopped stroking. "Perhaps you should tell me why you want to ruin a man's livelihood."

He groaned and lolled his head over so he could stare at her. "The man is an amazing butler. I would be stupid to get rid of him. But he knows he stepped over the line."

She resumed stroking his knuckles and he closed his eyes again. Men were more like cats than anyone had previously explained to her. "Does this have to do with the clue?"

He opened his eyes, the vivid green gazing at her again. "I almost called off the whole party. I was furious." His hand wrapped around hers, squeezing a little. "But Charlotte would be so upset if I did that and I don't think this is her fault." He picked up his empty tumbler and stared at it. "So here I am."

He had bottled up his anger. Then his solution involved opening a different kind of bottle. She asked, "Why didn't you find Charlotte and talk to her about this?"

He cocked his head to the side and stared at a spot on the floor again. "I would have had to show Charlotte the clue to explain why I was angry. That would have spoiled the game and I didn't want to do that to you."

His admission hit her hard and she gasped, clasping her hand over his.

He added, "Plus, I am a man. I do not talk to women about feelings."

She smacked the back of his hand. "You are talking to me right now."

"And I am getting assaulted for my effort."

He tried to pull his hand away but she clutched tighter. "I think I will hold you hostage until you tell me everything."

His lips quivered and he nearly smiled, but then it fell from his face. "You underestimate how long I can sit here. After all, I am not sober and can barely feel my rear end as it is."

She looked down.

"Are you looking at my rear end, Miss Locke?"

A warmth spread up her neck. "Should I not be? You are the one who brought it up."

He straightened a little, gripping his tumbler. Then he looked over at her and laughed.

She asked, "What is so amusing?"

"Is this the first time you have looked at my rear end?"

She opened her mouth then shut it. She said, "Of course it is."

He bent over, his forehead nearly touching hers, and whispered, "Liar." He let his head fall the rest of the way, nuzzling over hers. His eyes were closed again and his warmth enveloped her, heightening her awareness of her own body and the way it wanted to move closer to him.

He huffed a breath that reeked of brandy.

She pulled away and pushed his shoulders back, propping him back up against the wall. He accepted this handling and sighed.

She stood. "You complicate everything."

"That is unfortunate. My goal in life is to make everything as easy for myself as possible."

And that was the problem. He only ever thought about himself and how he could get the most out of any given moment. He would drink himself stupid on his study floor if that was what he wished.

She went to his desk to find paper.

Suddenly he was on his feet, behind her. "What are you doing?"

He maneuvered in front of her, blocking her way to the desk. She refused to step back and tried to go around him. "I need paper. And ink. And a quill."

He turned around and grabbed items from his desk. "This is my private desk. You cannot simply..."

He never finished his sentence, turning and handing her what she needed. She looked around him at his desk.

He was hiding something.

She met his eyes but he didn't deny it. He knew she suspected something. He said, "Tomorrow after breakfast. Another lesson."

"I do not think-"

His voice sharp, he interrupted her. "Tomorrow." A little softer he added, "I will be sober and a perfect gentleman. On my honor."

She accepted the paper he was holding out to her. "What room do you think the clue is referring to?"

He leaned against his desk, the sizzle in him a moment ago evaporating. "Will you look for the clue without me?"

"I don't know."

He grappled behind him for the decanter. She watched, feeling a little as if she had swallowed a small apple that was now stuck in her throat.

Or was that a feeling of building sadness she had to swallow down? Despite what everyone said about him, he wasn't a bad man. She wanted to believe he was selfish and obnoxious and a rake. And to a point, he was those things. But he didn't tell Charlotte about the clue because he hadn't wanted to ruin the game for her.

He had been thinking about her and wallowed in misery rather than reaching out to someone. She wanted to tell him that he didn't have to experience these feelings alone but that conversation was beyond her experience.

He poured a slosh of brandy into a new snifter and said, "It's my mother's room."

Chapter 14

Charlotte devised a game that Amelia had never heard of before. It involved beautiful paintings that were pasted onto wooden frames and then to make the game, some horrid individual took a sharp object to the pictures and cut each up into tiny pieces. Now the guests had to reassemble the pictures.

But that was not all. Charlotte was a fan of making things challenging. So the party was split, gentlemen against ladies, and they were to see who could first finish reassembling their picture.

Charlotte monitored the competition, gliding between the groups, checking on them, making small talk, sounding encouraging, and pointing out a piece if she saw something.

Amelia wasn't sure if she gave hints equally to the men and women and she didn't want to draw attention to it by asking. Charlotte had already helped her assemble three pieces.

Her mother sat across the table and made no move to even touch any of the pieces, but to her credit, she did sound encouraging whenever someone else managed to fit any pieces together.

Nina sat next to Amelia and had made the most progress on behalf of the ladies. She had an eye for spotting the colors in a brushstroke and Amelia wondered if the aptitude to reassemble cut pictures also extended to an ability to paint a picture in the first place.

Their picture, or so they were told, was of a yule log in a hearth. So far, there were brown and black pieces that seemed to be the log, gray pieces for the stonework, and red and orange colored pieces for the fire.

It was the last part that Amelia was tackling, trying to fit one reddish-orange piece to another orange-ish red one.

Next to her, Nina exclaimed, "Aha!"

For the most part, the women were quiet. It was the men across the room who kept erupting with things.

"Stick to the plan!"

"Henry, that is a red piece and you are doing the fruit bowl."

"Charlotte, are there dummy pieces? I can't make this one fit anywhere!"

Amelia was wondering about that last exclamation herself. She had come across a red piece that didn't quite seem to fit anywhere.

Nina leaned over and whispered, "I caught Charlotte in the hall before dinner. She was angry."

Amelia nodded. "Probably at Sudbury."

Nina turned a grayish piece and tried pressing it against another stonework piece. "What did he do now?"

How much should she gossip? Nina lived here and likely knew more about Sudbury than she did. She said, "He didn't want to join the party for dinner."

Nina snorted. "Drunk."

Amelia wasn't going to deny it.

Nina miraculously fit in another piece and Amelia had a sinking feeling that she was falling behind. The men were sounding a little too boisterous for her to hope they hadn't made much progress.

Nina whispered so quietly that Amelia had to lean in to hear. "I wonder if a woman here rejected him. It always seems to be a woman."

She was partially correct in her assumption. "I think he was upset about his mother."

Nina's piece slipped from her fingers, bounced off the table, and landed on the floor. She bent to retrieve it and whispered, "How do you know that?"

"He told me." That much was mostly true. He had said the clue bothered him and then later admitted something about his mother. She added, "I am his partner, after all."

Nina picked up the piece and straightened. "I suppose that is not a terrible reason for being indisposed. M-" she stuttered a bit and glanced around the table, "Mrs. Harris has said that he loved his mother very much and sometimes misses her."

Amelia was not above trying to glean more information. "He didn't say much about her. I wish I understood better because I am having a hard time forgiving him."

Nina glanced over at Amelia's pieces and slid her hearth section over, attaching it to a large chunk of fire. Then she slid the assembled piece to the center of the table.

In minutes, their group had assembled most of their pieces together and there weren't many pieces left. A silent, excited energy flitted through the women as they tried to hide grins and gasps of delight.

They didn't want the men to catch on to how close they were to finishing. Charlotte came over and caught on to the women's strategy. She silently drifted back over to the men.

Amelia fidgeted with one of the last remaining red pieces. It just didn't fit anywhere. The piece unnerved her and she had already squashed the desire to smash the piece randomly into a spot. Forcing it to fit somewhere it did not go wouldn't help them truly finish the puzzle.

The ladies all leaned in to stare at their picture. One piece was missing. Amelia held one red piece. She already knew it didn't fit.

Her mother snatched the piece from her and hissed, "Why are you hiding this? Do you want us to lose?"

She tried to push in the piece, angling it this way, turning it that way. It wouldn't go in no matter how hard her mother pushed.

Mrs. Harris leaned in. "That piece is not the right shade of red. It doesn't match the puzzle at all."

Irritation clawed at Amelia's patience. She had spent so long doing a miserable job of this and now all of their time was wasted because they didn't even have the correct piece. Their last piece. This wasn't fair.

Now the men would win.

She honed in on Charlotte, who had walked away from the tables to hold her hands up to the fire. She had her back turned on all of them as if she knew.

She did know.

Amelia stood up and put her fists on her hips. "Charlotte!"

Charlotte crossed her arms. "Yes?"

Everyone looked back at Amelia, waiting for her to respond. She felt every eyeball on her as if they were pins and she was the pincushion.

Sudbury added his voice to hers. "She's right! Now see here, you are funning us and it isn't fair."

The men couldn't finish their picture, either? She looked down at Nina, who didn't look upset at all even though she had done most of the work. Nina twisted around in her chair, her eyes bright as if she was ready to watch a good play.

Everyone looked between her, Sudbury, and Charlotte. They were focused on her and it felt like the sunlight making a warm alcove too hot. She swallowed, heat rising up her neck and cheeks and she knew her face was turning a garish shade of pink.

Charlotte quirked a brow at her. "Amelia, do you have something to say to me?"

She looked down at the piece she didn't remember picking up. It didn't match their puzzle. The men couldn't finish theirs, either.

Her thoughts were like the little pieces and she had just as hard a time trying to put them together. Everyone was staring at her and she didn't know what to say.

Sudbury called to her, his voice quiet and calm. "Miss Locke?"

She looked over at Sudbury, noticing that most of the men were looking at him, now. She knew what was wrong and she could fix this. "Do you need a red piece?"

He looked down and tapped his finger on something. "Yes."

Even though the attention from the group swiveled between her and Sudbury, she focused on him. If she did that, everyone else seemed to fade, the tension of being the center of attention pressing softer on her mind.

Sudbury picked up the piece the men had. "You are missing a red piece, too?"

She stepped forward and they met in the middle. She quickly assessed the brushstroke on the piece he held and nodded. He did the same. He moved to take hers but she held it firm between her fingers. "No. If we trade, fair and square, we finish the same way."

He didn't even look back at the table. Instead, his eyes held hers. Around the green of his iris, his eyes were red. He was here but just barely. He had shown up for Charlotte.

Something in the way he looked at her said he was here for her. She relinquished the piece and took the correct one, hurrying back to the table.

She counted, "One!"

She was aware that the party was watching them. Somehow, she managed to shove that aside, reveling a little in the giddiness tumbling around in her stomach. It was awkward to have everyone stare at her, but it was also thrilling to be the one to finish this.

Sudbury said, "Two!"

She held up her piece and he did the same, both of them bringing their pieces down at the same time. "Three!"

Charlotte clapped. "A tie! I was truly wondering how this would go."

Amelia wanted to glare at her hostess but she was trapped in Sudbury's smile as he stared at her from across the room. Of all the eyes that had been on her tonight, she didn't mind that his gaze had been one of them.

Chapter 15

It was tiring to hold onto secrets. The biggest one she had never received an answer to, a secret that she only held a piece of, had to do with Sudbury. When he entered her room that night, he had said her mother's name.

Not hers.

Not someone else's as if he had been in the wrong house.

Her mother's name.

And Amelia had never asked her mother what that meant. How would she bring it up? Oh, by the way, that night I kept a truth from you, I was wondering if you would share your truth because not knowing has been eating away at me like maggots eat at rotten meat.

Carrying secrets was disgusting, especially when it involved the people who were supposed to play a large role in your life.

Amelia promised to meet Nina later and excused herself from the breakfast table.

She entered the practice hall to find Sudbury pacing in front of a window. He looked up at her and smiled one of his winning, heart-melting grins of seduction.

She said, "When you look at me like that, I start to worry about what you are thinking."

"As you should!" Exuberant, he plucked out a fencing foil and handed her the hilt, then sunk into his stance and held up his own foil. "Today you will practice trying to take a whack at me!"

He was in an interesting mood today. She hadn't been sure what to expect after yesterday, but he seemed his normal, outgoing self.

She smiled and assumed her stance. Feeling bold, she teased, "You do know how to please a woman."

His eyes pierced her in a way that heated her core. She ignored her melting insides and lowered into her stance, foil up and ready.

They practiced a few defensive maneuvers and then he went over a stylistic technique to feint and lunge, her first offensive practice.

Now and then, she would try to whip past his defense, but he was fast and blocked her before she stood a chance.

She groaned in frustration. "I am never going to win this competition!"

"You need to school your expressions. I can tell every time you think you're going to try something sneaky because your eyes change and start darting around."

They practiced a bit longer before she tried another hit. If she couldn't look where she wanted to go, she would have to picture him in her mind and think there. It was difficult to concentrate on an imaginary Sudbury and keep track of the real one.

He still blocked her.

She complained, "I never get to feel like I'm winning. You are too good at this."

He lowered his foil and stood up straight. She realized her complaint made her sound like a petulant child and it was on the tip of her tongue to apologize.

Sudbury spoke first. "Amelia, I..." He stared at her but she didn't feel as if he looked at her. It was as if the smiling man from a few minutes ago had been a mask and now that was gone. "Do you know what it is like to feel as if you don't belong?"

She lowered her foil, stunned at his question. This real, raw Sudbury caught her off guard and it felt like he was due an honest answer. "All the time."

He raked his fingers through his hair and walked over to one of the tall windows, looking out. "My ancestors agreed to live and die for their king and country. That is why I have everything I do." He gestured outside. "I try to imagine this warrior, this soldier, this ancestor of mine who had killed and planned and plotted for his king, I try to imagine him settling in here. Did he feel as awkward as I do? Did he feel as if all this responsibility was a stifling burden instead of a reward?"

She could see it. She could imagine Sudbury in shining armor, racing across the country on a giant horse trained for battle. He wasn't just good at fencing. He was good at all of it. It fit him with a natural grace, this barely contained man of action.

He stared out the window and she wondered if he pictured the same thing, imagining himself riding free across the pasture. "I asked to leave. To fight for my country. I was told I had to stay here. I had to stay and take care of the parts of England that I am responsible for. For all of that, all of the people out there, all the crops, the animals, the tenant houses, the parish, I was trapped."

He was so still, she wanted to put a hand on his shoulder. He barely looked at her when he added, "I had lost my mother shortly before I went to London. Nothing was keeping me here, anymore. I went *bad*. I turned my back on my home and lost myself in a city that wanted whatever I felt like giving. I did what a better man would never have done."

Back during her season in London, he had been notorious. He had been the bad man, the rake, the wolf among sheep. He had acted as if he didn't care about anyone else. But now she wondered if his truth was that he hadn't cared about himself.

Afraid that if she spoke too suddenly or too loudly, she would scare him away, she murmured, "You are not in London anymore."

He clenched his fists. "I can't change the past." He looked over at her, his green eyes haunted, and she could almost see his memories rolling past like paintings in his mind. "All I can do is change who I am now. I can be here. I can perform my duties. I can try to be at least a shadow of a gentleman. But inside, there is still a part of me that feels trapped. Stifled."

"You want to be free."

So did she. She stepped up next to him by the window.

He turned and brushed his fingertips over a few strands of hair near her forehead, pushing them back. "I am not trying to make my life of wealth and privilege sound as if it is not good enough. I thought over many things yesterday and I think I understand why you want to go to Greece."

She didn't know what to say.

He added, "There is something about you that you do not want me to know. I have not figured it out, yet. You, by no means, owe me your secrets, but," he brushed his fingers against her cheek, "there is a part of me that wants you to be happy."

Secrets. She did have secrets and he was at the heart of some of them. Did he even remember? He had never brought it up and she wasn't sure if she should ask. The questions would form in her mind but she wasn't certain if the words would ever come out of her mouth.

She wanted to know.

Along with knowing came a streak of fear. If he remembered, how much of a pit did that knowledge put between them?

Or worse, what if he didn't remember? What if she was just part of another forgotten liaison in a year of bad decisions?

She thought of the clue in her pocket. The one that had caused him so much trouble. She asked, "Are you willing to work on the next clue with me?"

He pulled his hand from her face and stepped away. "Yes. I will not let you down."

Chapter 16

If his partner had been anyone other than Amelia, he wasn't sure if he would be in his mother's room.

Amelia cleared her throat and he looked over at her, her hand pushing aside the window curtain. The window was covered to protect the room from sunlight. Even though it was daylight outside, they needed a candle to chase away the shadows.

He said, "If there is something you want to say, just say it."

She skirted his mother's bed and went to the small escritoire. He winced at the sound of scraping wood as she opened it.

She said, "The clue mentioned a tragedy. In the book, the heiress's body is found in her bedroom so I am just trying to think about her, er, body in the room."

He stared into the flame of the candle. "Where was the body found?"

She paused from rifling through his mother's papers, something he wasn't sure anyone had touched in a long time.

He should definitely fire his butler.

She said, "I just said her body was found in her bedroom."

He set down the candle because he feared he would hurl something at the wall. This room evoked so many emotions and he didn't want any of them. Shoving his hands in his pockets, he relaxed his jaw so he could grind out a few words. "I mean where in the room was her body found? The bed? The floor? Slumped in a chair?"

Amelia winced and he wasn't sure if it was because she was picturing a dead body in the room or if it was because of his tone.

She thought she wanted him here.

Here he was.

She knew he didn't want to be here.

Softly she said, "On the floor."

He scanned the floor. The quicker they found the clue, the sooner they could leave. "Doesn't the last line of the clue say something about treading carefully?"

She took the slip from her pocket and then nodded. "It does. That must be a clue."

He snorted. "Obviously it is. The entire shoddy poem is a clue."

Her eyes widened and she slipped the paper back into her pocket. Silent, she turned around and began inspecting her corner of the room.

He pinched the bridge of his nose. His mother's perfume bottle was still on her vanity and her mirror had dulled with age. This room was all that was left of her and it stood here stuck in time.

He should definitely fire his butler.

He opened his eyes to find Amelia crawling on all fours, pressing against the wall trim. "What on earth are you doing?"

"Sudbury?"

Had she found the clue? Could they leave now? "Yes?"

"Was she awful? Is that why you don't want to be in here?"

"Awful?"

She pressed against the next section of trim. "Your mother."

No. His mother had been wonderful. She was the opposite of awful, whatever that meant. Whatever words expressed how wonderful a mother she had been, he tried to reach for the right thing to say. No one should ever think she had been anything other than a perfect mother. "She loved me."

Amelia, still down on all fours, stopped inspecting to look over at him, her eyes blinking as if she needed a moment to focus her gaze. "Oh."

He felt something scratchy in his throat. Heat built behind his nose and eyes and he turned away from her to take a shuddering breath. Shakily, he said, "I suppose I miss her still."

Amelia stood. "As you should."

He covered his face with his hands, trying to hide the onslaught of emotions that were rolling through him like a building storm.

No one else had ever loved him like his mother had. Not even close. It was dubious whether his father had loved him at all. His various family members, his cousin, his uncle, none of them had cared about him on a level that even neared her love.

But his mother, she had truly loved him. He hadn't been an easy child but she had been there for him, believed in him, scolded him, and made him better. Ever since she had gone, he hadn't been the same man.

No one had cared about her passing as much as he did.

His problem had been in the fact that he had ever experienced love at all.

The loss of her love had felt like the end of the world. Like a man in the desert whose canteen just ran out.

And he had tried to figure out a way to keep living. He had not only tried, he had thought he had succeeded.

But that night, standing in Amelia's room, something had itched at him. A feeling. He wasn't even sure what feeling, but he had a feeling and it had felt like an itch that couldn't be scratched.

Not necessarily love, but something honest and clean and worthwhile.

Sudbury thought his friendship with Henry had changed him. Feeling valued by someone for a reason other than his literal monetary worth had felt...

Nice.

And in slow ways, Sudbury had made decisions to change. He didn't have to be a rake. He didn't have to be a scoundrel. He didn't have to be less than a person.

But he had never entered his mother's bedroom again until now.

He remembered the smell of her perfume. He remembered her checking her hair in that mirror. He remembered how beautiful she had been in those gowns.

He remembered how empty it felt to lose her love.

Amelia wrapped her arms around his waist and rested her head on his shoulder. He pulled wet hands away from his face and held her, soaking in her comfort like a dirty rag.

He needed to get himself in check.

She asked, "Has anyone ever told you that love cannot die?"

Her hair tickled his face and she was warmer than he thought she would be here in this unused room.

She pressed on. "I mean it. My grandmother was the one who used to read to me. When she passed away, I was devastated. Probably the smartest thing my mother has ever told me is that my grandmother's love stays with me. Just because she is gone, doesn't mean she has taken her love away."

Love was something stupid and intangible. It made idiots like him leave tears in the hair of pretty women. He wiped his cheeks before he could do any more damage.

She asked, "Would you like to tell me about her?"

He cleared his throat. "She could see a constellation out her window and decided before I was even conceived that she would name her first son after those stars."

She muffled her response against his shirt. "Orion."

He turned his head and breathed in the citrus scent of her hair, pressing his lips against the top of her head. "Yes."

She said, "I will probably never be able to look at those stars now without thinking of you."

He hugged her tighter against him. "You think of me when I am not around?"

She quietly laughed. "You mean like when you're late and I wonder where you are?"

He dropped his head further down hers, trailing a couple of soft kisses down her temple. She closed her eyes and he heard her take a deep breath. His lips against her cheek, he said, "That is not quite what I meant."

She clung to him. "Sudbury."

She wanted him to kiss her. He knew that. And he wanted to do it, everything in his body told him to move down a little more.

But a tiny, functioning bit of his brain reminded him that he was standing in his mother's bedroom.

Slowly, he relaxed his arms. She opened her eyes and before he let go completely, he explained, "We need to find that clue."

Chapter 17

I t had been under the carpet.

If she stopped to think about the book, the location of the clue made perfect sense. The body of the heiress had been found on the floor in the middle of the room and the clue had said to tread carefully.

As soon as they had the clue, Sudbury bolted.

He muttered something about a job well done and then disappeared around the corner.

It had been obvious that he struggled to be in his mother's room. Something about it made him appear raw, his eyes red, his body stiff, his manner abrupt. He had been very different from the lazily amused Viscount he normally was.

He had felt like a real person and it unnerved her to think of him that way.

Sudbury the rake, Sudbury the rogue, Sudbury the gambler, Sudbury-the-man-who-was-always-late. These were the ideas of him she had in her head. But Sudbury the vulnerable, Sudbury who was loved, Sudbury-the-man-holding-back-tears, these were all versions of him that tugged her in a different direction.

She had been overly critical of him because of his reputation. People saw her as Amelia-the-wallflower, Amelia-the-bluestocking, Amelia-the-book-reader,

Amelia-the-quiet-one, and she knew she was more than those things. It was unsettling to realize that maybe she had been too quick to judge Sudbury, just as so many were quick to write her off as a mousy nobody.

They both deserved more.

This new way of understanding Sudbury made her see him as a man she could grow to like.

Why did she feel as if they could be friends?

His emotions. They made him feel real, and if he could have real feelings, then he was capable of other things, such as friendship.

If he wasn't the rake, the gambler, the ne'er-do-well all the time, then that left him open to being trusted. She was starting to see what Henry and Charlotte saw in him.

He was amusing, he could be considerate when he wanted to be, and he wasn't all that bad. Maybe what he needed was more good in his life. It was easy to make bad decisions and it was easy for one bad decision to lead to another.

It was hard to make a change for the better. Sudbury hadn't done that alone, he had found a friend in Henry to help him. And now he was friends with Charlotte.

And maybe, if she thought about it, he was friends with her.

She liked spending time with him.

Except, she had to admit, because that inner voice that constantly whispered things on the inside of her head, that voice that knew no lies or secrets, it told her there was more to Sudbury than friendship.

She secretly wanted all of him.

While she was being completely honest with herself, she also still wondered about that night. Had he been there to meet her mother? That was something that hovered over their interactions. His past hit her on a personal level, close enough that he affected her family.

Amelia had learned long ago that her mother's motivations were not always inspired by Amelia's best interests. It wasn't that her mother wanted to hurt her, it was that she had never had to stop to think about anyone but herself. Whatever maternal instinct that some women claimed to be born with had skipped Amelia's mother.

So what had been the motivations behind that night? Why had Sudbury entered her room? Had that been a mistake? Or on purpose?

By the next morning, after breakfast, Amelia worked up the courage to ask him. That was the only way to find the answers she wanted. She could either confront her mother, which she knew would be pointless, or she could ask Sudbury.

If he remembered that night.

At his closed study door, she listened to the muffled voices before knocking. One was low and female and the other voice was definitely his.

The female voice spoke again and the muffled tones locked into her memory, the voice fitting into place. It was her mother.

Sudbury and her mother were together in the study.

She glanced down the hall to make sure it was still empty, then moved her ear near the latch of the door. Her mother spoke but Amelia couldn't make out the specific words.

Sudbury's quiet rumble was much clearer. "What would she think about it?"

Amelia felt her heartbeat quicken. She was listening to a private conversation. If it involved any two other people, she would pull back and leave. But she couldn't. She had to know more.

Most of her mother's response was too quiet but she did hear, "...really like..."

Sudbury's response was also partially muted, but she heard, "...think...beautiful..."

If Sudbury and her mother carried on with a secret relationship, neither of them would tell her. The idea was just as shocking as finding them here together, but the voices on the other side of the door were indisputable proof that the two were having secret meetings.

Is that why her mother had agreed to come? She wanted to make up for that night long ago? Maybe they were going to pick up where they had left off.

Amelia pulled her head back, swallowing hard against the saliva building in her mouth. She sucked in a deep breath through her nose, hoping it would calm her roiling stomach.

She had carried her lies for so long. She had lied to her mother about Sudbury. She had lied to her father about that night.

Had that been the right thing to do? If she had told her father somehow about Lord Sudbury's interest in her mother, if she had offered even a partial truth, would anything have changed for the better?

Amelia knew her mother to flirt, but never more than that. If her mother was practiced at keeping secrets, if she could keep them from her husband, it stood to reason she could be discreet enough to keep them from Amelia as well.

She didn't doubt for a moment that Sudbury would carry on with an affair. She knew she couldn't trust him and that he was prone to bad behavior.

He was a rake, after all. He was only doing what everyone already suspected.

And it hurt.

Just yesterday she had felt sorry for him and now the betrayal snaked through her, leaving behind a poison that left her gasping.

She needed to get away. Stumbling down the hall, she braced herself at the entryway and, her legs feeling like jelly, she dropped to a bench. Anyone walking by would see her but she had to breathe and calm her shaking before she could take another step.

Footfalls down the hall drew nearer and she hoped it was only a maid, preferably with an armload of linens so she wouldn't even see Amelia on the bench.

Her mother cried, "Amelia! Whatever are you doing here? Are you ill?"

At moments like these, when her mother's usually apathetic manner was occasionally set aside, when she stopped long enough to think of anyone beyond herself, Amelia had to face the fact that this was her mother.

She wanted her mother to care about her.

Even though she so rarely got what she wanted.

Her mother put a hand under Amelia's arm. "Can you stand? Otherwise, I will call a footman."

Amelia stared at the floor and swallowed, wondering if she would be sick right here on the beautiful marble. The swirls on the floor made her head spin and she squeezed her eyes shut.

Another voice. Sudbury's. "Mrs. Locke? Am..." he hesitated, "Miss Locke?"

These were the last two people she wanted around her right now.

Her mother said, "I don't think she can stand. Could a footman carry her to her room?"

"A footman?" Sudbury sounded offended.

Amelia felt arms around her body. She opened her eyes as Sudbury lifted her off the bench and carried her up the stairs. She swallowed again, the motion upsetting her stomach, and she groaned.

He whispered, "If you cannot hold it in, you will not be the first woman to cast up her accounts on me."

They were nearly to her room and she found the breath to mutter, "You probably deserved it."

He stood aside so her mother could open the door. "I probably did."

Chapter 18

Christmas was a few days away but after a day of ice skating and warmed beverages, the guests were full of good cheer.

Amelia adjusted her wool shawl around her shoulders and eyed the smiles around the room. It was hard to feel quite the same way when the best part of ice skating was getting to come back inside and warm up. She would much rather have sat by the fire and read a book.

As the company sipped their drinks and the rosy cheeks faded, Amelia noticed the butler exchange a few words with Charlotte. The conversation was quick. The butler silently bowed and withdrew.

Charlotte clapped her hands. "Someone in this room has an announcement!"

The room quieted and glances were thrown about as guests tried to surmise who would speak next.

Her brother raised his glass and gestured with his arm to her. Startled, she blinked and then frowned at him. What did he want with her?

Next to her, Nina stood. Laurence hadn't been pointing at Amelia at all. He had been gesturing to his partner in the game.

Did that mean?

Could they have?

No.

No, *she* was supposed to win. She was so close.

Just the other day, Nina had told her how behind they were with the clues.

But Amelia had given the answer away. She had been right there, about to check underneath the bench. All Nina would have had to do was become curious enough to come back. She wouldn't even have had to figure out the answer to the second clue.

Laurence raised his voice to carry about the room. "Our final answer was submitted for approval and we have just found out..."

He looked to Nina and let her finish. Nina, in a pretty, long-sleeved gown of pink satin, clasped her gloved hands together in front of her, her eyes shining. "We solved the final clue and are the first to have finished the mystery game!"

They won. Her fingers numb, Amelia clapped along with the rest of the guests. She even tried to smile but the odd, twisted feeling on her face probably looked as awkward as it felt. She couldn't hide the sinking feeling of misery that pressed like a dank fog inside her, It was unfair.

She should have known that their team would pose a challenge. After all, she knew Laurence had read the book. And Nina, an unabashed novel reader who had been bonding with Amelia for days about books, would have thrown herself at this game with a similar tenacity to Amelia's.

But no one here could feel the way she felt about losing. Declaring Laurence and Nina the winners made everyone else the losers.

Amelia left the others even though it was in bad taste to do so. Tears blurred the stairs as she ascended and made for her room where she could be miserable, alone, and a failure.

She made it to her room and tried to close her door but a hand and foot stuck in the way. Wiping tears away from her cheek with the back of her gloved hand, she sniffled and said, "Mama?"

Her mother entered the room and shut the door behind her, then removed her gloves and sat on Amelia's bed, patting the spot next to her. "Amelia."

She remained standing. "I want to be alone."

Her mother patted the spot again. "I know. I also know you wanted to win that game and you are upset about it."

Astounded that her mother would notice anything outside of herself, Amelia's other emotions suspended for a moment while she wondered what to do about this attention.

She said, "I worked really hard. I truly thought I would win."

Quick and succinct, her mother said, "Yes. I know."

Likely her mother's interest in someone else was fading and she would leave in a minute. Amelia would just have to ride out that minute at her mother's whim.

Her mother blinked slowly and said, "I know why you wanted to win."

Amelia found a square of fabric. "I know you do not like to travel."

Her mother waved off that comment. "No, not that reason. I *know* why you wanted to win."

She clutched the fabric in her fist. "Mama, what do you mean?"

"Amelia, you are my daughter. You live with me. We do not necessarily spend our days together, but your life is not as much of a secret from me as you think it is."

Her fingers began trembling and a fresh set of tears tingled behind her eyes. "Mama?"

"I read the book. Your book. *The Mystery of the Heiress.*"

She was losing feeling in her hands and parts of her body started to feel as if they were parts of a different person. As if her own legs belonged to someone else because she wasn't sure whether they would keep her on her feet. "All the women were supposed to read it for the party but I did not think you would."

"Because I do not care to read. But I did read *your* book. Not only did my daughter write a book, but she got it published. Of course I read it."

"Mama."

She wasn't sure what else to say. The hot tears behind her eyes leaked forward and new, fat, wet drops blurred her vision again. She sniffled and brought the bit of fabric up to wipe her nose.

Her mother said, "I liked it. If it had been, perhaps, a play or something less taxing on my eyes, I would have enjoyed the story immensely."

Immensely.

Not a regular type of enjoyment.

Immense enjoyment.

Her mother nodded and fresh tears streamed down her cheeks, more sobs shaking her body. Laurence was the only one who knew she had published a novel because she had needed his help to do so. He had contracted with the publisher for her and helped her set up her payments.

Her brother's support had meant the world to her but she never, ever expected anything from her mother. She had, if anything, expected criticism, admonishments, or even anger.

This moment of acceptance felt like a tunnel had cracked open within her and from it, new feelings could flow. Her mother had never cared about anything Amelia did, much less going out of her way to show her support.

She asked, "You're not angry?"

Her mother said, "I am upset that you have kept this a secret from me."

What about the past? What about those secrets?

It was too much.

"Mama?" The silence stretched and she went on. "I want to know why we cut my season short so suddenly."

Curt, she answered, "I thought you were relieved to leave."

"I was. But some things happened that do not make sense."

Her mother's voice grew colder, closing her off again. "What things?"

She was reverting back to the woman who only wanted to worry about herself. Soon, the conversation would end with how tedious it was and Amelia wouldn't get any of her answers.

She asked, "Why was Lord Sudbury outside our house that night? It did not feel like a coincidence."

Sharp, her voice slicing, she said, "It wasn't."

"Why was he," Amelia licked her lips, "causing trouble? He said something," she tried to rally her thoughts and assemble a coherent sentence that tied all of her caution and frustration together, "about you. He said your name and that he was there for you."

Her mother crossed her arms, something she would never do because it could wrinkle her dress. "You are just bringing this up now?"

Slowly, she admitted, "I didn't know what to think at the time."

"And what do you think now?"

"I..."

She couldn't say it.

Her mother uncrossed her arms and gripped the edge of the bed. "I see."

In the quiet, Amelia waited. Her mother could get up and leave. This conversation could have pushed them even further apart. She hadn't realized how badly she wanted the approval of her mother until she was on the brink of losing it.

She stumbled to the chair in the corner, dropping into it so heavily that the legs scraped along the floor.

So quiet, like a ghost whispering from the bed, her mother asked, "Do you remember Lady Edderdown?"

Almost as quietly, she answered, "Yes."

This conversation was fragile. Her mother was about to share something that she had never shared before and if the moments in their lives had gone any other way, this conversation might never have taken place.

But now it was going to.

Her mother said, "I could have gone that season without her acquaintance."

Amelia sifted through memories of the lady. She had always dressed in the height of fashion, always wearing decadent accessories such as rare feathers, carefully placed jewels, and expertly painted fans. There had never been an inch of the woman that let anyone doubt her title or her wealth.

Mother had hated her.

She asked, "How does Sudbury relate to Lady Edderdown?"

"All season, that woman and I had played," her mother paused a moment, seeming to reach for the words she wanted, "little games with each other. I would contrive to rip one of her hems. She yanked on the delicate gold of my diamond necklace. I poured red wine down her reticule and she spread a rumor about me. You can see, I am sure, how these games grew."

Amelia stifled a strangled sound in her throat, not daring to say a word.

"I suspect that Lord Sudbury was a part of those games. Whether he was knowingly conniving with Lady Edderdown, I cannot say." From across the room, their eyes met and Amelia was surprised to see the misery in her mother's expression. "By that time, not only were you thoroughly ready to return home, but so was I. Sending men to my home was a bit beyond where I was comfortable playing the game."

At home, her mother was known as an entitled, albeit untitled, woman who was worth her credit. Father was extraordinarily wealthy but money could not buy social status in a system that was rigged by the royalty. Amelia had met a duke who rubbed in her face how close to the throne he was.

Literally, he had told her how many people would have to die for his pompous personage to sit on the throne.

That kind of thinking created a rift between people who may or may not deserve to sit on a throne and the people, like her father, who had worked hard to build his business into something of his own empire. Amelia had never fit with anyone her family had tried to socialize with in London, but she had also never stopped to think about how the rest of her family may have struggled as well.

Her mother thrived on attention. And even though Amelia had faced rejection after rejection, she had expected it, even felt relief at it. But her mother?

It would have strained her to a point that matched the misery written right now on her face. Amelia stood and crossed over to the bed. She sat, the mattress sinking under her weight and her mother shifting to accommodate her.

Her mother took her hand between hers. They were very different people and that was something Amelia had accepted. She still cared for her mother.

And, with a quick, affectionate squeeze of her hand, she felt that her mother also cared for her, in her way.

Her mother said, "I do think I approve of Lord Sudbury. I was not sure of his character before, but now I suppose he is not quite the man the gossips have made him out to be."

Amelia, trying to hold back the acidic affliction in her tone, said, "I do not think the gossips were far off from the man he once was."

Her mother pulled her hands back, resting them in her lap. "I think the man he was to the gossips and the man he is here and now are perhaps not quite the same man. The previous man was an interesting topic of conversation but the current Lord Sudbury is a man I have not minded conversing *with*. There is an interesting difference between those two men."

Dryly, she said, "He is interesting. I will give him that."

Her mother rose from the bed. "I think we will see more of Lord Sudbury in the future."

With that puzzling pronouncement, her mother nodded at Amelia and left the room.

Chapter 19

Sudbury handed her the fencing foil. She had spent her last practice completely immersed in her technique.

In other words, she had completely ignored him. He would call out a suggestion and, although she made adjustments per his comments, she never verbally responded to him.

She was angry.

He shouldn't care. The old Sudbury wouldn't care that she was angry. He would leave her alone and consider it a good thing that she didn't want to speak to him. It would have been a relief.

It was not relieving to be ignored by Amelia. He had been finally living in color these past weeks and now every time she rejected him, a little bit more of that color leeched away.

He wasn't worth her time. He wasn't worth her.

At least not when she was angry.

That was about how his life went. Every time he found something he wanted, it was taken away. He loved his mother; she was gone. He wanted to fight; he was denied. He had a splendid time at a house party; it ended like this.

He found a new friend; she left in anger.

He knew that people accused him of being callous, of using them for his own amusement, of being a thoroughly awful human being.

It was hard to be anything else when that was what he felt. Awful.

If Amelia wanted to compete while holding onto her anger, then he wouldn't stop her. Fencing wasn't about emotions and they would only get in her way.

She would lose the competition just as they had lost the mystery game.

Amelia's first match was against Emma. He heard the beautiful heiress had enjoyed learning some basic moves but had not thrown herself into it with Amelia's tenacity. But with her anger crippling her judgment, he wasn't sure whether Amelia's extended knowledge would be an advantage.

Amelia on the left and Emma on the right, the women took their places, foils up. If Emma had only learned the basic movements, she learned them to perfection. There was nothing he would change about her stance.

Amelia, however, was leaning forward too far, too eager to pounce. Starting sloppy would only deteriorate her technique from here and he slid his hand down his face, squeezing his eyes shut.

He didn't want to watch this.

He wanted a good swig of brandy and for someone else to help him forget to care about absolutely anything.

Next to him, Amelia's brother said, "You said she was doing great at her lessons."

"She was."

Go away, go away, go away. Unless this young pup had a hidden flask somewhere, Sudbury didn't care to talk to him.

Laurence winced at Amelia's first advance. She was leaving herself wide open while she attacked without any precision. "I guess I thought..."

Sudbury clenched his fists. "She has been angry ever since you won the mystery game. You're her brother. Why am I the one telling you this?"

His anger seethed and rippled down his skin, his entire body taut. He didn't want to be here. He didn't want to watch this. He didn't want to have this discussion. He wanted Amelia to do better because he knew she could.

If she lost this, she would only retreat further away from him.

The elegant and very precise Emma slipped her blade inside of Amelia's shoddy defenses. Amelia shuffled back, narrowly missing the touch.

He called out, "What are you doing? Get your blade in front of you and mind your angles. It's not a broadsword!"

Laurence, clearly having lost his wits, remained by Sudbury and said, "Why would Amelia want to win that game? She shouldn't have even been playing." He was quiet for a moment while Sudbury reeled at that comment. "Besides, she doesn't want to travel. She likes being at home."

Sudbury sputtered, "She likes..."

He tried again, "You think..."

This is what he wanted to ask. "What do you mean she shouldn't have been playing?"

Laurence shifted his weight away and avoided his gaze, intent on the match.

Sudbury tore his eyes from the face of the man he desperately wanted to pummel.

Emma was slow and careful, but Laurance had taught her a solid defense. Amelia, her movement hurried and clumsy, tried to hold Emma's tip aside and slide her blade in. Emma circled Amelia's foil and pushed her blade to the outside, forcing Amelia to step back and quickly bring her defense back up.

Laurence said, "My sister is going to have to be smarter than that to get past Emma."

Amelia's back hand that was out for balance was a tight fist. Her movements were getting more and more jagged as the match went on.

She tried the same tactic, this time with a feint. Sliding her foil down the inside of Emma's, she was almost there. Sudbury leaned forward.

Emma swirled her foil again, pushing Amelia's back to the outside, but this time she slid her blade forward and her tip touched Amelia right in the middle of her chest.

Sudbury's uncle called the point and, one lady stiff, the other graceful, they shook hands.

That was it. Her first match and she had lost.

SHE HAD PLANNED TO arrive at a Christmas gathering, eat a few extra sweets, quietly watch the fun of the evening games, and then return home.

Sudbury had ruined that. From the first day, he had lured her to his side and began the downward spiral that anyone foolish enough to follow him must take.

She had jumped. Why? Because he was handsome. Because she had been curious. Because a part of her wanted the things that he dangled in front of her.

She had been stupid to think that she could do anything outside of her comfortable life. Fencing. Games. Feelings.

Kisses.

She stalked away from the guests and down an empty passageway. If no one stopped her, she might very well keep stomping all the way to her room. To her traveling dress. To the carriage. Down the road.

All the way home.

She wanted all of this to be over.

She was so stupid. She had thought if she feinted, she could sneak her blade in. This competition would only prove how inexperienced she was and how pointless it had been to try to teach a group of women to fence in only two weeks.

She would take years to be as good as Sudbury.

His voice called down the hall, echoing. "What the hell was that?"

He thought he was angry? Her own furious turmoil rose like a rearing stallion and she desperately hoped to trample anything in her path, especially Sudbury.

She threw down her foil, having nearly forgotten she was still holding it until it clattered to the floor. It bounced and rolled away, the tip turning and pointing at her accusingly.

He strode forward. "You are angry. At me."

"I am angry at everything!"

He stopped, the foil between them. "You can't win without a clear mind."

She flung her hand out to gesture to the competition hall. "I have already lost!"

He took a step forward. "The first match only. If you win the next two against Nina and Charlotte, then you make it to the final round."

She laughed. Win both matches when her first had been a disaster?

He took another step forward. She took a step back.

He took another step.

She stepped back.

He grabbed her shoulders and backed her up until she was against the wall. He said, "I trained you. I know that you are capable of winning. I am telling you that if you stop acting like a spoiled, sullen brat, then you can win."

"Excuse me?"

"Or are you going to run away?"

His question hung between them. She had wanted to run away.

He hovered over her, trapping her against the wall, preventing her escape. Quietly, he said, "I am surprised at how easily you gave up. I had thought you more of a fighter than this."

She was a fighter.

She had spent most of her life feeling lonely and rejected. She had never had many friends as a girl, she hadn't known how to make them at the ladies academy, and she had never gotten over that hurdle when her mother thrust her into the thick of a London season.

That had been it. Her entire existence as an heiress had been to get married and she had failed.

It had been a relief to leave London, but it had also left a hole inside of her that she filled with a sense of failure and hopelessness. Who was she if she could not fulfill the roles that were expected of her?

She wasn't a wife so she couldn't be a mother. She wasn't very good at sewing or companionship. She was a quiet, dowdy woman with a pile of books.

So she had embraced that. Who was she? A lover of books. They became her life.

So much so that she wrote one. She had agonized over the rough draft, plot points, who her characters were, and what they wanted. She had wasted paper rewriting new, better drafts.

Then, her nerves a jangled mess, she handed the culmination of her life's worth over to her brother.

That was it. Her entire life had boiled down to the book in his hands. Would he like it? Would a publisher like it? Would readers like it?

If they didn't, then everything she had dedicated herself to had, once again, been pointless.

She would go back to being a dowdy spinster with a pile of books and no real use to anyone.

Her back against the cold wall, Sudbury put his arms on either side of her, leaning forward. His green eyes caught hers and they sparkled with a heat that she felt all the way down her spine.

The wall behind her wasn't so cold anymore.

He asked, "Why should you not have played the mystery game?"

She swallowed. What did he know?

His breath raked across her cheek. "Amelia?"

She turned her head to the side and his lips hovered over her temple, tickling her and sending tiny shivers over her shoulders as he said, "You have a secret."

His lips, so soft they felt as if he was dragging a rose petal over her skin, dipped down the side of her face and over her cheek. His fingers touched her chin and he turned her head to face him.

No, not to face him.

His lips dragged over the corner of her mouth and settled, petal-soft, over her for a kiss.

Chapter 20

This luxuriously soft press of his lips sent sensations cascading from the top of her head down to her knees.

She leaned harder against the wall. His arm wrapped around her back and he tilted his head, somehow finding a way to press each sensual plain of his body against hers. She tingled in places she didn't know could feel so alive.

He took in a deep breath through his nose and whispered her name, "Amelia."

He had promised that kisses didn't have to have an end and she wasn't ready for this one to stop.

She tilted her neck up and stretched up to him. If he was surprised, his body didn't show it. His mouth moved to her bottom lip, pressing tiny kisses along the outline of her mouth.

"Ryan."

He paused with his mouth over her top lip. "What did you call me?"

"Ryan."

"No one has ever called me that."

She was aware that her chest rose and fell as if she had been running. "I think, when some women are in the throes of passion, they say 'Oh' a lot. Shall I call you, 'Oh, Ryan'?"

He laughed and rested his forehead against hers. "How would you know so much about a woman in the throes of passion?"

Her arms wrapped around his back, her hands coming up by his shoulders and she held him close, taking in the scent of his starched shirt and a soft hint of musky cologne.

"Amelia?"

"Yes?"

He pressed his lips against her forehead and then pulled his head back to look at her. "What if I stay with Henry and Charlotte for a bit? Then I will be close enough to properly court you."

All sense left her head and she knew her mouth was open, her tongue left with nothing to say.

He went on, "I will send you flowers. I will send you sweets. I will send you as many books as your heart desires."

"You want to *court* me? As in, court, the thing men do when they are interested in marrying a woman."

His fingers tangled in hers. "Yes. I realize that you will leave in a few days and I am lamenting being alone in my own house."

His hands felt divine twisted in hers. "But Mrs. Harris and Nina live here, too."

He kissed her cheek. "I am trying to say that I will miss you."

"Oh."

She turned her head and kissed just under his ear. He made a rumbling sound in his throat that sent a ripple of pleasurable triumph through her body. She kissed again in the same spot, then tried exploring a few other places down his neck.

His voice raspy, he asked, "Does this mean you would like me to follow you?"

If he followed her, they would have to discuss things. They would have to talk about that night. She would have to tell him what she did with her time.

Who she really was.

She said, "A few minutes ago I was very angry. But I don't think it was fair that I was angry at you."

He held still and didn't respond. It was probably the wise course of action.

She went on, "I am sorry that I assumed you to be all the things that everyone else sees you as. I should know that the person everyone else sees is not always an accurate view of who that person truly is. And, I think, back when you wanted us to be friends, I was too hasty to assume you saw me in the way I am used to being seen."

He pressed a little closer to her, confining her body between his own and the wall. "And now what do you think?"

She drew in a deep breath, her chest brushing against his now that he was so close. "I think I misjudged our friendship and that you have been a better man than I initially saw."

Something lit in his eyes and his focus darted around her face. He stepped back. "I think you should go win your next two matches because if we don't leave this hall right now, I will ravish you."

⚜

DESPITE HER STRONG defense, Emma lost her other two challenges.

Charlotte had a lot of energy, but she was playing for the fun of it and only won her match against Emma.

The last match was against Amelia and Nina. Amelia had won one match and lost one match. Nina had won both of her matches. If Amelia lost this, Nina would be declared the winner of the competition. If Amelia won this round, then Amelia and Nina would be tied and would move into a second round to determine who was the actual winner of the competition.

Amelia had never played for anything so serious in her entire life.

She put on her protective mask and clarified that last thought. Other than publishing a novel, she had never done anything so serious.

No wonder men did these kinds of things all the time. It was thrilling. It felt powerful. If Amelia had a sword at her side and came across a criminal vagrant, she could vanquish him.

Every woman should be taught to fence.

Sudbury stood down a way on Nina's side of the fencing strip. If Amelia struggled, they had worked out some hand signals for tips and suggestions. If he thought she should strengthen her defense, or try a feint, or convey a weakness, Sudbury would be there for her.

She trusted that.

She moved into her stance, foil up. With Emma, she had been too hesitant, too nervous to make the first move. Now she just wanted to win and that would never be accomplished by standing and waiting.

Mrs. Harris yelled, "*Allez!*"

Amelia advanced, closing the distance between herself and Nina. Her opponent held firm, foil up, ready to defend.

Nina clashed her foil inside Amelia's, a simple attempt to knock her defense aside and slide her blade in for a touch.

Amelia stepped back and twisted her tip around to push back Nina's blade. She jumped forward quickly and pushed her foil in.

"Touch!" cried Mrs. Harris.

Wait. What?

Was that it? It was over?

"Miss Locke wins. We will take a brief break and then come back for the final match."

She had won that round? Already?

She looked over at Sudbury's wide grin, his arms folded over his chest and his eyes telling her *I told you so!*

He had believed in her.

She pulled off her mask and rushed over. "Now what? I don't know how I did that. It happened so fast."

He brushed a lock of her hair behind her ear and she realized that they were in a room where everyone could see them.

Heat rose up her neck and she whispered, "Sudbury."

He whispered back, "I thought I was 'Oh, Ryan.'"

The heady feeling of victory swirled around her head, her body heated from the exercise and excitement. She wanted him to kiss her, to feel all of the things coursing through her right now.

That playful light danced in his eyes and he knew it. He knew what she wanted.

He said, "Nina has quick feet. She can advance and retreat faster than you. But your blade movements are faster which is why you won this round. Nina is going to come back determined and better prepared because my cousin is not an idiot and he will give her good advice."

He stopped talking and she waited in the silence. And waited. Finally, she said, "Well? What is your good advice for me?"

"Nothing. You have good intuition and your instincts have won you most of the rounds because the technique I have helped you develop is solid. Nina is good. So are you. She has quick feet but you can use that to your advantage. I would tell you to get her moving and get her to focus on her feet so you can sneak in with your quick blade, but that is exactly what my cousin is telling her that I would tell you. So she will probably be expecting that."

Amelia's shoulders tensed, straining with frustration. "So my advantage is not an advantage at all?"

"You can still follow your instincts. You are still quick with your blade. You will see your moment when it comes. And," he leaned closer and whispered next to her ear, "even if you lose, I still plan on kissing you senseless at my first opportunity."

She glanced around to see who could have overheard that bold statement. Everyone was giving them space, probably assuming Sudbury was giving her advice on her next match.

No one was listening.

She stretched up as if to whisper something but she pressed her lips at that spot under his ear. Then she suddenly pulled back and said, "This is it! Wish me luck."

His eyes followed her with the sense of a lurking panther and he said, "It is I who am supposed to give you the token of good luck."

She retreated a few steps back. "Too late now. I will have to make do with what I have."

She could do this. She could win. Sudbury believed she could and, well, if she didn't, she still had a successful published novel, a secret identity as an author, and the promise of mind-melting kisses.

She put her mask back on and raised her foil.

Mrs. Harris yelled, "*Allez*!"

Nina held still. Amelia advanced. Nina held firm, holding her blade up for a strong defense. She looked determined not to let Amelia through.

Suddenly, Nina whipped her blade in, forcing Amelia back. Nina was faster, already advancing, pressing in closer, forcing Amelia to retreat farther to try to get her defense back in place.

Nina thrust her foil to Amelia's left, and it nearly would have been a hit if Amelia hadn't retreated another step. She couldn't keep giving up ground.

Another step back and Amelia decided to ditch her defense. If Nina thought she would press on in a rapid and steady offense, Amelia would use her faster blade.

Or so Sudbury claimed it was.

And she trusted him.

She whipped her blade forward and up, catching against Nina's foil and forcing it up and out of the way. Nina tried to pull her blade back but Amelia was already there to tap it again, forcing Nina's blade back and also Nina herself as she scrambled to bring a defense back up.

It was too late. Amelia couldn't stop her advance. She was completely consumed in the moment, in the movement of her feet, in the tap of her foil and the sensation down her arm as she held the blade just so, her fingers ready to guide her to a precise win.

She would win.

Nina jumped and then quickly fell forward into a lunge, trying to pass quickly beyond Amelia's foil for a sudden hit.

Amelia, by sheer luck, already had her blade ready to parry and she held Nina's low lunge aside while she slid her own blade to the right and deftly twisted it in for a hit on Nina's side.

"Touch!"

Mrs. Harris's voice echoed throughout the room, or maybe it was the moment echoing in Amelia's head while her mind tried to haul itself back to reality. She pulled off her mask and someone took it from her hands. She shook Nina's hand, realizing her own was shaking.

She said, "Thank you. Thank you so much."

Thank you for giving me this win. Thank you for having been a good friend during this house party. I am sorry that I was a sore loser before. I hope I can make that up to you.

Amelia held all of these things inside for later.

Nina grinned at her. "I plan on forcing Mr. Sudbury to continue training with me. Now that we've started I can't possibly stop."

Amelia smiled back, relieved at Nina's easy friendship. "We will have to continue getting together for practice challenges."

Nina winked. "I look forward to beating you the next time we do this."

Amelia turned to Charlotte and Emma who had closed in to offer their congratulations. Her brother pulled her into a giant, utterly brotherly hug of which she had no escape and he told her how proud he was of her.

Sudbury was last in line to offer his congratulations. He held her head gear and foil and, despite the neutral tones of his voice, his eyes twinkled with a promise that left her heart thudding in her chest.

Chapter 21

The house smelled of the earthy, tingling scent of greenery. When everyone woke tomorrow it would be Christmas Day and Charlotte had a handful of activities to keep everyone busy, concluding the day with a small Christmas ball.

As long as everyone celebrated Christmas and only Christmas, he didn't mind what Charlotte had planned.

He did not want anyone to celebrate his birthday.

He didn't want any toasts or well wishes or recognition. He didn't need anyone to remind him that he had wasted another year with debauchery and selfishness.

He was a changed man, but not completely changed.

He opened a bedroom window. The wind whistled past the house, stinging his cheeks. The upper story ledge wasn't icy, or so he hoped. Otherwise, his fool heart would be smashed on the ground and he wouldn't worry about tomorrow at all.

He just really wanted to do this one thing.

Gripping the windowsill, he tested the ledge with his shoe, sliding his foot back and forth to determine if it was slippery.

He swung his other leg out. This was it. He was climbing out on the wall of his own home, like some sort of thief or wastrel. But he was only one of those things.

Holding onto the wall, he shifted his feet over and over and over, trying not to look down and slowly testing the next strip of the ledge for any slippery spots. His fingers quickly began to ache, even through his gloves, as the cold seeped in and the wind stole the warmth from his cheeks and nose.

Almost there.

She had the curtains pulled closed. He paused at the window, listening for voices.

Even the wind had calmed for a moment, letting him take in the complete silence of the night. He sucked in a frigid breath and then lifted the window.

It stuck and his heart thumped on the double. He was going to be stuck out here and have to scoot all the way back to the other window. He gave one more push, gripping the frame like his life depended on it. It shifted, the frame made a cracking noise and then opened.

He tumbled in, rushing in so fast that he landed with a grunt on the floor.

He blinked and glanced around the room. The quiet form on the bed didn't move. He could leave his packet of papers on the desk and be out of here in a blink. He didn't relish the thought of going back out the window, but now that he was here he didn't have another option.

He stood.

The figure on the bed moved. She rolled off the bed and darted to the fireplace, snatching up the fire poker.

He held his hands up. The low glow of the embers illuminated the outline of her body against the white cotton of her night rail. Someone help him; she had no idea how delectable she looked brandishing a poker.

He said, "You have much better form this time."

She rubbed at her eyes and straightened. "This time? Sudbury?"

He asked, "May I lower my arms now?"

Slowly, she lowered her weapon and he rested his arms, the papers still clutched in his hand.

Her voice sweet with the rasp of sleepiness, she asked, "What are you doing here?"

He held up the papers. "I was pretending to be Father Christmas. You were supposed to be asleep and wake up to this in the morning."

She set down the poker and then held out her hand for the papers.

"No, no. These are a Christmas gift to be opened tomorrow."

She crossed her arms. "Why? I am not a child."

He raked his eyes up and down her figure and softly said, "No. You are not."

He hoped she was blushing.

He said, "If I set these on the desk, will you wait until tomorrow morning to look at them?"

"Probably not."

"I value your honesty." He tucked the papers back into his coat.

She reached a hand forward. "Well, wait!"

He waited.

She pushed her braid behind her shoulder and bit her lip. "What did you mean when you said, 'this time?'"

"The last time we were in this situation," he motioned his hand between the two of them, "your form was awful. If I had been a true threat, I would have just knocked aside your poker and had my way with you."

"Excuse me?"

He couldn't imagine a man seeing her this way and not wanting to have his way with her. On the bed. On the floor in front of the fire. "Is now a good time to kiss you senseless? I think I promised that."

She said, "You remember that night?"

Of course he did. It was scorched into his mind and no other woman between then and now had ever removed his memory of her curves under her night rail, of her hair mussed around her head, of her face sweetly blinking with surprise.

Rather like she looked right now.

He said, "I remember it as if it happened yesterday."

She crossed her arms. "You asked for my mother that night, you cad."

He winced. "I had been misled."

He didn't remember that entire night. He remembered little key moments that led up to Amelia, but most of the night was fuzzy and he doubted the accuracy of his memories, this many years later.

She whispered, "Lady Edderdown?"

"How-how did you know?"

She shrugged.

He stepped forward. "My life changed that night."

Her eyes met his and he took another step, resting the backs of his fingers against her cheek. He meant his words about that night. He had met Amelia who had shocked him and embedded herself into his memory. He had met his best friend Henry who encouraged him to be a better man. He had decided that he would never be misled by Lady Edderdown ever again.

He said, "Sometimes, when I wondered whether I should slip back into my old habits, I would think about the people I had hurt. For some reason, if I imagined that person was you, I couldn't do it. Whatever bad habit tempted me, I ignored it by asking myself, 'What if this person was Miss Locke?'"

She nuzzled against his fingers, the velvety, sensual feel of her cheek feeling like the skin of an angel. Almost too good for the likes of him.

She wrapped her hand around his wrist, trapping his hand where it was. With her eyes closed, she said, "My life changed that night, too."

He had to clear his throat to check that it still worked. Somehow he managed to whisper, "It did?" She had him completely entranced. He slipped his arm around her waist and pulled her close. Now they were both trapped. "Tell me."

She licked her lips, tucking them into her mouth while she thought. He wanted to lean forward and kiss his way up her chin, teasing her lips back out so he could nibble on them.

She said, "That night felt like an adventure. The next morning, it almost felt as if it had happened to someone else. For a little bit, I pretended..."

She trailed off and his imagination filled in all the things he wanted her to pretend. And a lot of the things he definitely did not want her to fake.

She went on, "I felt like a character in a novel. Like I had lived through a little bit of a story. So I started wondering what kind of a story would involve someone sneaking out the window. How did that story start? Where did it go?"

His hand slid up the side of her face and his fingers spread into her silky hair. "If anyone knows about stories, it would be you."

Her eyes widened. "I began writing it down."

His eyes drifted from her hair over to meet her gaze. "You began writing down a story?"

She licked her lips again and nodded.

"And before that night, you had never written a story?"

She shook her head, her hair running delightfully around his fingers. She said, "I had written short stories and poems. But this particular story..."

Was this what it was like to be a changed man? To care about another person? He wanted to know how she would finish that sentence. He wanted to know what she was hiding and he wanted her to know that she could trust him with whatever it was she had to say.

He said, "Unless this story led to murder, there is not a single way you could finish that sentence that would change how much I love you."

She stilled.

He thought she had been still before, but this was different. Nothing about her moved except the beat of her heart. For a moment, he wasn't even sure she breathed.

Suddenly she sucked in a breath. "Ryan, I..."

He dipped his head forward. "If you don't finish your next sentence, I am going to consider this conversation past the point of reason and begin to kiss you senseless."

"I think I love you, too."

He felt his chest cave in as he exhaled but it was hard to suck in a new breath. The weight of those words crushed in on him and he knew with his next breath that he would never be the same way again.

All   at   once,   she   said, "Iwrotethenovel*TheMysteryoftheHeiress.*"

Her chest heaved and he watched it pump up and down while he tried to process her words.

Slowly, he said, "You are A. N. Neemus."

"Yes. I wanted to remain anonymous."

He kissed her. He couldn't not do it. He barely realized that was what he was doing until his lips covered hers and she moaned against his mouth. His body melted on the inside and hardened on the outside as he held her against him.

He kissed the corner of her mouth. "You have..."

He kissed her cheek. "...a secret..."

He kissed by her ear. "...identity and..."

He kissed over her temple and then dragged his lips back down her cheek, kissing as he went. "... I have never..."

He slid his mouth down her neck. "...felt so much passion..."

She moaned when he kissed the spot where her neck met her shoulder. "...for anyone else, ever. You are almost like a spy and I have never found a secret identity more thrilling."

Her hands dug into his hair and she said, "I am nothing like a spy. That is all in your imagination."

He laughed. "All in good time, my sweet."

Chapter 22

She woke early, the morning still looming somewhere beyond the horizon. It was still very dark in her room but she knew it might feel a bit more like Christmas if she stoked the embers back to life. She just needed a bit more warmth and light to feel like today was special.

It would be special anyway. There would be games and a ball and the pudding she had waited all year to eat.

In the glow of the rekindled fire, she noticed the packet of papers on the desk. Sudbury must have left those after he had tucked her into bed. She picked up the stack and carried them over to her bed, snuggling back into the covers to peruse the sheets.

There was a contract for the services of a companion signed by Mrs. Pepperidge.

Then there were tickets reserving a private cabin for the staggering price of one hundred pounds.

But that wasn't all. There were letters extending lines of credit.

And finally, a letter from the mysterious Mr. Day, inviting her to stay at his villa.

This packet was everything she needed to travel to Greece.

This is why he had acted so strangely when she wanted to fetch paper from his desk. He had been hiding these. Even then he had been thinking about her.

This represented Sudbury's effort at a truly thoughtful Christmas gift. A gift for her.

She sniffled and felt warm tears in her eyes as she picked up the sheets again, glancing over each one.

There weren't any strings attached to this gift. He hadn't asked to go with her. He hadn't asked for anything in return. He had thought only of her and providing her with something that meant the world to her. Now she could go explore, have an adventure, see somewhere new. She wasn't going to travel via book.

She could go see what she wanted, do what she wanted, be who she wanted.

Amelia the explorer. Amelia the dancer. Amelia the writer.

A maid entered the room and blinked at her. "Miss, are you feeling well?"

Amelia blinked, too, trying to clear the tears from her eyes. "Good morning and happy Christmas."

FOR THE FIRST TIME since she had arrived, he saw her wearing something that wasn't completely horrendous. Her gold silk skirt flowed from a fitted bodice with pink beading, a delicate color that matched the soft pink in her cheeks.

She looked happy. She looked beautiful.

He asked, "Did you open my present?"

She reached out her gloved hand and squeezed his arm. "Ryan, I cannot express enough gratitude for the gift."

He looked down and realized his other hand had covered hers and he didn't remember moving his arm. "Are you going to continue writing about your heroine's escapades in Greece?"

She moved closer so their conversation wouldn't be overheard. "Oh, no. I think I will have to write about a new heroine. This one knows how to fence and solve mysteries and..."

She trailed off, the ideas taking root in her mind.

"You cannot keep doing that. You must finish your sentences because the suspense kills me."

She giggled. "There might be kissing in the next book. Whoever this new heroine is, she might fall in love."

He wrinkled his nose. "A romance?"

She nodded, smiling and confident.

He led her closer to the dance floor. "I suppose a love story is not so bad if it involves fencing and a bit of mystery."

"Ryan?"

He looked over at her, tucked next to him, so perfectly. "Yes?"

"Is there a way you could come with me?"

"Go with you where?"

She stopped walking and glanced around at the guests. She whispered, "To Greece."

His fingers threaded through hers. "There is a way I could come with you but you are ruining my plans. Remember I was going to woo you with sweets and new novels."

"Oh." She bit her lip. "Is there a way you could save the wooing for later? I would rather have you sooner than that."

He coughed and sucked in a harsh breath. "Have you?"

She scrunched her delicate brows at him. "Yes, go to Greece with me. Why are you looking at me like that?"

He wrapped his hand around her waist and hauled her closer to him. "I am trying very hard not to kiss you senseless in the middle of my ball."

She glanced around at the guests, pushing at him and giggling. "You cannot hold me this way! It is very inappropriate!"

He smirked as the first notes of a waltz lilted around the room. "Dance with me?"

She smirked back and placed her gloved hand in his. "For your birthday, I suppose I will."

Epilogue

Amelia tapped her fingers back and forth on the paper-wrapped package.

The butler knocked, opened the door, and announced a guest. "Lord Sudbury."

She squealed and bounded up from her chair. "Ryan!"

The butler bowed and left the door open. Ryan grinned at her and quietly shut the door anyway. He swept her up in his arms and planted kisses across her forehead. "My dear, this would be easier if you weren't holding an inadequately sized shield between us."

She wiggled away and held up the gift. "I know you haven't read it, so this one is for your eyes only."

They sat together on the settee and he unwrapped the book. Opening the cover, he read the inscription out loud, "To my love, from Amelia Locke." He looked up at her and asked, "Is this the only book signed with your true name?"

She nodded, relief flooding her that he understood how important this was. She was giving him something that meant she trusted him implicitly, even with her biggest secret.

He picked up her hand, encasing it between his own. "I will keep this in my bedchamber so it is for my eyes only until and unless you are ready to change that."

Chapter thirty-five, the chapter that involves escaping out a window, was dear to heart and she wanted to flip there and point it out to him. She tried to pull her hand back to point at the book but he held her firm.

Captive.

He gazed into her eyes and it felt like he was staring not at her new dress (which he had not yet commented on), not at her blush, not even at her mouth as if he might kiss her. No, he stared at her, his gaze peeling back all the layers until he saw the woman. A desirable woman whose hand he would not, could not relinquish.

"Amelia."

"Ryan."

If only he would just kiss her and dispel the tension.

"Will you marry me?"

She couldn't breathe. She wasn't sure, her body did it so often without thinking about it, but now she was very aware of the lack of breath coming into her lungs. Finally she said his name. "Ryan?"

His hands tightened around hers. "I am a changed man, Amelia."

She leaned forward and placed her free hand over his. "You don't have to change who you are for me to love you. I think the person I love has been inside of you this entire time."

He huffed. "That does not at all answer my question."

She brushed a kiss over his lips, watching the way his long lashes fluttered over his cheeks. Against his mouth, she murmured, "Of course I will marry you."

He nuzzled against her temple. "So we will get married. We will travel to Greece. Then you will write another fantastic novel that will sweep through the drawing rooms of the world."

She laughed. It felt so good to be loved. "And?"

"And," he tapped the book in his lap, "your secret is safe with me."

AUTHOR NOTE: THANK you so much for reading! If you have a moment, I would appreciate a review from a reader like you!

Other books in the series: Miss Moore's Christmas Scandal

Printed in Great Britain
by Amazon

34424796R00098